TERROR FOREST

SEE MORE AT
WWW.COLLEENHLAVAC.COM

TERROR FOREST

COLLEEN HOFSTADTER HLAVAC

SEE MORE AT <u>WWW.COLLEENHLAVAC.COM</u>

Instagram: @colleenhofstadterhlavac

Facebook: @Colleenhofstadterhlavac

Email: colleenhlavac@gmail.com

To Lauren, Jason, Olivia & Sara, my four children, who have given me a lifetime of joy, love and support.

1

DEAL, NEVADA

Chants rose into the hot, summer night air like helium balloons escaping their confines. They raised their arms and chanted in unison.

A makeshift altar had been set up in a grove of redwood trees. They appeared to be in a trance-like state. Standing in a crescent moon configuration, they were all dressed in black.

An exceptionally tall, cloaked figure in a dark robe led the ceremony. Candles perched on top of the altar illuminated his outline.

As with every ceremony, near the conclusion, a special tea was distributed to all of the members. A symbol of a mushroom was etched onto the side of the kettle.

After the ceremony concluded, the leader, Abbott, announced updates to the members of the cult.

"I'm not liking our numbers one bit. We haven't added any new members in some time. I understand that living in the small town of Deal limits how many newcomers we can find. But, we've got to step up our efforts. We need to thrive and ultimately become the rulers of the world. Let's mainly focus on recruitment right now. Another thing, sacrificing Belle London was simply stupid. She was way too high profile of a person. Think about it, folks. You kill the homecoming queen of Deal High School, and we all suffer the consequences. You started a frenzy with law enforcement. They're asking a lot of questions. Now, there's even going to be a crime documentary show about Belle's death. This is the kind of attention we just didn't need!"

Abbott adjourned the meeting and the members silently slithered off into the undergrowth of the dense Nevada forest.

LINDEN, NEW JERSEY

Winter Wells sprung up from her desk as the final bell at Linden High School rang. She exited the building feeling a combination of excitement and nostalgia.

Her long, wavy, caramel colored hair bounced along her back. Winter's crystal blue eyes blinked away the harsh, afternoon sunlight.

She had just completed her junior year. It was finally summer vacation!

The beautiful, fun-loving teen had lived in Linden, New Jersey her entire life. Recently, her minister father, had received a job offer he could not refuse. Mr. Wells was hired to be the lead minister in a church in Deal, Nevada. Unlike his current job, he would now also hold a supervisory role.

Winter turned to her best friend, Jules.

"I'm so proud of my dad but I still can't believe we are moving as far away as Nevada. That's clear across the country! I've been friends with you since preschool. I'm going to miss you so much."

"I can't believe it either. I'm going to go through some major withdrawal symptoms without you. I've been begging my parents to look for jobs in Nevada so we can move there too. Mom and Dad look at me like I'm crazy whenever I suggest it. They've both been working at the same jobs for the past twenty years. But, you just never know. Stranger things have happened. I won't give up. I'll keep pushing them."

"I'll keep my fingers crossed. I just can't imagine starting a new school and you not being there."

"I know. If all else fails, I guess there's always FaceTime. We can talk every single day. It's almost like we'll be in the same town. And, I can come visit during Thanksgiving break. Dad already promised me that I could."

"I'd love that so much. Who knows? Moving to Deal could end up being the start of many interesting adventures."

2

DEAL, NEVADA

They emerged from the shadows. Hooded cloaks revealing only their soulless eyes. The murmur amongst the cult silenced as the leader, Abbott, stepped up onto a rotten tree stump. He removed his hood and his teeth snarled in fury.

"You fools! I warned you not to kill without my approval."
The leader spit into the crowd.

His rant continued."Guess who paid me a visit this afternoon? Sheriff Booker! It appears that Mrs. Brownson was found slaughtered in her chicken coop this morning. It's pretty obvious to me that one of you clowns did this. I've told you over and over again to clear every act of violence with me first. Now, I have the heat on me! Who among you killed her?"

Abbott grunted and glared out at his group of nervous followers.

At first, there was complete silence and clear hesitation on the followers' parts.

Then, twelve of them all pointed to the same individual.

The leader's anger rose to dangerous levels. He took a lead pipe from his bag and hit the guilty party on the knee cap, shattering the delicate bones.

None of the members reacted to the violence. They were used to Abbott's rages.

To say he was a hot headed, power hungry man, would have been an enormous understatement. It was understood to never cross or disobey him.

Abbott predicted who the guilty party was before the members even pointed him out. This particular man served as a constant sore spot for him. He was always pushing the limits and testing Abbott. No amount of discipline had managed to make him more obedient.

3

LINDEN, NEW JERSEY

Winter had never been to Nevada before. In fact, prior to the move, she had not ventured further west than Michigan. Throughout childhood, her family would spend a month every summer at the Sleeping Bear Dunes National Lakeshore on Lake Michigan.

Hiking the wooded trails and playing on the beach were among her most treasured childhood memories. The ten hour car ride felt eternal to Winter.

Now, in retrospect, it was a stone's throw away compared to driving to the state of Nevada.

Winter was born and raised in New Jersey and prided herself on being a true Jersey girl. Other than googling images of Nevada on the internet, she had no clue what to expect.

Not surprisingly, her best friend was unable to convince her parents to move to Deal. It was just Winter, her parents and their cherished pets.

Yukon, a lovable Saint Bernard and Bumble, a tenacious and adorable Corgi, would accompany them on their new adventure.

Winter was an only child. To her parent's dismay, they were unable to conceive after she was born. Her mother was diagnosed with endometriosis. Despite surgeries and other fertility treatments, they were unable to have a second child.

In order to ensure that Winter had plenty of companions at home, she had always been blessed with a house full of pets.

The Wells family arrived in Deal just before sunset. Winter had been quiet during the final hour of the car ride but, finally, she interrupted the silence.

"Can't believe we're finally here. That was one heck of a long trip. Are we almost at our new house?"

Her fatigued father responded. "Should be there in about three minutes. I think you'll like the house. It backs to a forest and it's only a short walk to your new high school. We even have a hot tub!"

Winter's father pointed. "Here we are now! That's the house!"

"The one with the long driveway, Dad?"

"Yes, honey, exactly!"

The driveway meandered up to a two story, brick home.

The house had seen better days. Weeds filled the front lawn and the baby-blue front door was in desperate need of a fresh coat of paint.

"Don't worry, ladies! We'll get our house looking good as new in no time."

Jan, Winter's mother, a chronically optimistic person, chimed in, "I can see that it has a lot of potential, honey. I love that it's surrounded by Ponderosa Pine Trees."

Winter's mother had received her graduate degree in Forestry at U.C. Berkeley. There wasn't a plant or tree that she was not able to identify and she was happiest when she was wandering through forests. The move to Deal was a dream come true for her. The terrain was much more wooded than their former home.

"Until we get the yard fenced in, we'll need to keep an extra close eye on Yukon and Bumble. In the meantime, there are acres of wooded terrain around our new home. Plenty of room to take the boys on walks. Should keep them from getting too restless."

"Sounds like a plan, Dad. I'll make sure they get plenty of exercise so they don't go stir crazy."

The following morning, the family of three crowded around the kitchen island and enjoyed their Saturday breakfast tradition, Eggs Benedict. A piece of ham tumbled to the floor and their favorite vacuum cleaner, Yukon, gobbled it up.

The Saint Bernard was known, in the family, as having the ability to spot even the smallest crumb of food. Jan often joked that he did a more thorough job of cleaning than the Roomba and a cleaning service combined.

After breakfast, the doorbell chimed. Jan answered.

Moments later, she returned with a teenage girl in tow. Winter gauged the visitor to be around her own age. The girl was substantially taller than Winter, at around 5'9. Her platinum blond hair fell into soft, bouncy layers.

Jan cleared her throat. "Winter, this is Jenna Booker. She lives next door."

"Hi, Jenna, It's nice to meet you."

"If you'll excuse me, girls, I have a zoom meeting starting in a minute." Jan exited the kitchen.

"Could I get you some breakfast?"

"No, thanks. I already ate. I just wanted to come over and introduce myself. I know it can be hard moving to a new area at our age. I just moved to Deal four years ago. It took some getting used to, that's for sure. What grade are you going into?"

"I'll be starting my senior year. I was born and raised in New Jersey. Had the same friends all my life. So, this move is definitely nerve-wracking for me."

"Don't be nervous. First of all, we are in the same grade. I'll be a senior too. Also, I have a big group of friends here. I'd love it if you'd hang out with us. We can all even walk to school together on the first day."

"Oh, wow, I'd love that. Thanks so much."

"Of course, it's no problem. Hey, I need to get going but would you like to come to Hals with us tonight for dinner? It's our favorite pizza joint around here."

"Yeah, I'd love that. Thanks!"

"Why don't you come over to my house at around 7:00 and I can drive us there."

"I'll be there. I'm unpacking all day, so, that'll be a perfect time for me to take a break."

4

Cosette was slumped over her desk battling another wave of nausea. As if on cue, Tommy, her co-worker and best friend, walked over and handed her a cup of ice. "This will help."

"It always does. You've got to be the greatest friend in this entire universe."

"I'm thinking that award goes to you, Cosette."

Cosette was currently near the end of her first trimester in pregnancy.

Luke, her fiancé, catered to her every moment that they were together. As a homicide detective, Cosette worked long hours at the Reno Police Department. Tommy was very protective of her.

Whenever, she looked fatigued or felt uncomfortable, he would dote on her.

After sipping on ice, Cosette's nausea instantly subsided.

Just then, Tommy's father and head of the homicide unit, Frank Munro, marched into the room.

"Cosette, Tommy, let's have a quick meeting. Trouble is brewing in Deal, Nevada. That's a town in Douglas County, about forty miles south of Reno. It's really close to the town of Genoa "

"What's been going on, Dad?"

"Some very brutal murders, that's what's going on. Deal always had a close to zero crime rate. That's, unfortunately, changed. The sheriff, Todd Booker, called me this morning. He sounded pretty anxious. Told me that a high school student by the name of Belle London was brutally murdered one night on the high school's football field...Now, an elderly lady and pillar of the community, Ruth Brownson, was murdered and dismembered in her own chicken coop. Booker told me it was the most brutal scene he had ever witnessed in all his years in law enforcement. Obviously, the citizens of Deal are scared out of their minds. Booker doesn't have the manpower to work on these cases alone. He asked if I could send a couple of my people to help investigate. I brought you some files about the murders. Brush up on the details today. Then, I'd like both of you to head down there tomorrow morning."

Frank placed a thick stack of paperwork onto Cosette's desk.

"Let's dive in, Tommy."

"I'll get us some coffee. This is going to be a long day."

DEAL, NEVADA

Winter walked over to Jenna's home. Her new friend was already waiting in her crimson-red Audi Convertible. Her hair was swept up into a casual ponytail... perfect for driving with the top down.

"Hey, girl. How did your day of unpacking go? You must be beat!"

"We barely stopped all day. Amazing how much stuff we accumulated over all these years. Can't wait for our new place to actually start looking like a home. I'm exhausted. A night out is exactly what I need."

"I think you'll really hit it off with my friends and the pizza there is the best. Try the Maui Zaui. People say it's every bit as good as Chicago pizza."

The friends whisked off in the sporty car and arrived at their destination soon after.

"This place sure is hopping!"

"Always is. It's the go-to place for our town and even for the surrounding towns. The lot is full…as usual. I'll park down the street and we can hoof it."

Jenna whipped her car into the first spot she found on a residential street and they walked to Hals. Flashing neon, red lights framed the restaurant. Jenna greeted the hostess. They clearly knew each other well.

"Hey Jenna. Your gang is back at the usual table."

"Thanks, Gigi."

Behind the hostess stand, Winter noticed a poster of a striking teen. The caption stated, *In Memory.* Her curiosity was piqued and she turned to Jenna.

"Who's that?"

"That's Belle London…was a super beloved girl in our high school. Our group was good friends with her."

"Was?"

"Yeah, she was murdered on the school's football field not too long ago. We're all hurting!"

"Seriously? How awful! Did they find the killer?"

"Nope, not yet. Now, there's been a second murder in town. Sweet Mrs. Brownson. The cops aren't releasing details of how both of them were killed. Rumor around town has it they were axed."

A feeling of terror engulfed Winter. This was the first she had heard of the heinous crimes.

"That's creepy. Of course, there were crimes where I moved from. Linden is right next to the city of Newark and close to the Big Apple. So, I'm used to hearing about murders but two homicides in such a small town is a whole different story."

"They'll catch who did it. My dad is the sheriff of our town. He doesn't even tell me the details of the murders, but, he did tell me that some fancy homicide detectives from the Reno Police Department are coming into town to help him crack the cases. Dad's good at what he does but two murders is more than any sheriff can handle alone."

Before Winter could ask any more questions, Jenna led her across the restaurant.

Winter was introduced to Jenna's group of friends. They were welcoming and kind to her.

"Guys, this is Winter. She just moved here from New Jersey. Lives right next door to me. She'll be in our grade at school."

A gregarious teen was the first to chime in. "Hey, Winter! I'm Zarina. It's great to meet you. Have a seat. You've got to try this pizza. It'll erase all the homesick feelings you have."

The group of friends laughed. It was clear to Winter that Zarina was the leader of the group. Confidence radiated off of her as the others huddled around her. Her jet-black, wavy hair moved as soft as prairie grass in a spring breeze and her brilliant, white smile served as a striking contrast to her golden skin tone. Mint-green, electric eyes were lined generously in onyx. Zarina's artificially long lashes batted flirtatiously as she scanned the boys in their group. They all appeared enthralled with her.

Winter noticed Zarina's striking necklace. "I love your necklace. Is it rose gold?"

"Aw, thank you. It is rose gold. My grandmother gave it to me on my sixteenth birthday. The angel pendant is supposed to always protect me. I never take it off."

"Well, it's gorgeous. Your grandma has great taste."

Winter took a bite of the food. "You guys weren't kidding. This pizza is insanely good."

Zarina nodded in agreement. "Right? I can't get enough of it. Hey, guys, haven't we been here long enough? I'm stuffed. After everyone is finished eating, let's head to the barn!"

Winter raised her eyebrows. "What's the barn?"

Jenna chimed in. "Zach lives on a farm just outside of town. We love hanging out in his barn. It's cool. I think we have enough booze hidden under the hay to get an entire army blitzed."

The group laughed uproariously.

Winter felt uncomfortable but pushed herself. Being a child of a minister, she had always made a point of avoiding alcohol. She quickly reminded herself that it was important to fit in since she was the new girl in town.

5

The group of friends caravanned to Zach's home. He lived in a sprawling, ranch-style home out in the country.

The sky was velvet black with only a sliver of a moon clinging like a silver claw in the atmosphere. The darkness felt oppressive, almost supernatural to Winter.

A blanket of stars seemed to stretch to infinity. Bats grazed hungrily at mosquitos around the only streetlight on the country lane.

As they parked and trudged towards the barn, sorrowful sounding coyotes could be heard howling off in the distance.

With flashlights illuminating the way, they entered the paint chipped, poppy-red barn. The sliding doors stood open. The group kicked dust in the air causing Winter to stifle a cough. Shelves were covered with boxes.

A group of goats stirred from their slumber. Zach zeroed in on Winter. "These are my pets. They're light sleepers, only sleep about five hours a night. The poor guys get woken up by us every weekend when we come here to party. They're real characters."

The goats sprung up eagerly to greet the group.

"They're a lot less grumpy than I am when I get woken up." Winter was pleased to elicit laughter from her new friends.

One of the goats made a bee-line for Winter. "She's a friendly one."

Zach agreed. "Yeah, she sure is. That's Daisy. She has a love addiction. Can never seem to get quite enough attention."

Winter instantly liked her.

Zarina pulled up a section of hay from the corner of the barn. "Bottoms up. I don't know about you all, but, I'm ready to get hammered."

They all helped themselves to Jack Daniels. Zarina turned her head to Winter. "Here, girl, have some."

Masking any hesitation, Winter thanked her and took the disposable cup. She sampled the potent liquid. It scalded her throat but she proceeded to drink. Not being used to drinking alcohol, she felt the dizzying, heady sensation soon after her first sip. Winter got home way past her curfew that night.

DEAL, NEVADA

Cosette and Tommy had pored over all of the details of the murders in Deal. The next morning, they drove the forty miles to the sheriff's office.

Sheriff Booker's office was housed in a small room within Deal's town hall.

Cosette knocked on the sheriff's door. A man with shining, energetic eyes, bristly eyebrows and a hawk-like nose swung the door open. His warmth was infectious. The easy to love gentleman welcomed them into his modest, untidy office.

"Welcome, friends. You must be Cosette and Tommy? Can't quite tell you how 'ppreciative I am that you're giving me a hand. This is a doozy of a case. Frank told me he gave you the files on both murders. Have you had a chance to peruse them?"

Cosette responded. "We sure have. There was a lot to unpack but we feel pretty polished up on the details now. Your files were very thorough, Sheriff."

"Appreciate that. I try. These murders have me terribly stumped. Other than both homicides being carried out with an ax, the victims have little in common. Belle London was a popular high school girl and Ruth Brownson was old enough to be Belle's grandmother. Both ladies were adored in Deal, so, they have that in common. Otherwise, they're completely opposite. Belle's murder happened at night. Ruth's happened during the early morning hours when she was in her chicken coop. Do you think we have a serial killer in our midst, folks?"

Cosette cleared her throat. "It's too early to determine that, yet, Sheriff. The fact that both of the victims were killed with an ax makes me think the same person or people did both of the homicides. There was only one set of footprints in the chicken coop. Frank believes that there was just one killer involved in Ruth's homicide. He isn't quite as sure with Belle. There was a football game a few hours before her slaying. Needless to say, there were countless footprints all over the field. As you're aware, the coroner determined that the assailant was left handed based on the angle of the entrance wounds on both victims. Since only ten percent of the U.S. is left handed, it makes it all the more likely that the same killer was involved in both murders."

Tommy scratched his chin. "One of our tasks, while we're here, is to set up a StingRay. It's a device that allows us to track people's movements. We'll also be able to intercept and record conversations, text messages and names from mobile devices within your town. I feel confident that if someone in Deal is the guilty party, we'll figure it out. Before we begin, is there anyone in town you want us to keep a particularly close eye on…a trouble maker, someone with a police record?"

"There sure is, folks. Two gentlemen come to mind. Kurt Tomlin is Belle's ex-boyfriend. He's a few years older than she is. They were together for over a year. Belle dumped him about two months before she was killed. Word around town is that he was completely blind-sighted and destroyed. Kurt would show up wherever Belle was and he'd text her at least twenty times a day begging for her to take him back. She'd block his number and he would just figure out the new number. He has a tendency to get into bar fights. So, I know he's prone to violence."

Cosette inputted the information. "Ok, we'll be on the lookout for him. I'll try to interview him later today. You said there were two men to look out for. Who is the second one?"

"The second one is Blade Florence. He's in his late thirties. Blade was born and raised here. He drifts in and out of town but he was in Deal during both of the murders. Scum bag got arrested twice for beating his former wife. It happened over ten years ago but any man who raises his hand to a woman is the lowest life-form. That behavior doesn't expire, in my humble opinion."

Cosette scanned her notes. "Tommy, why don't you have a chat with Kurt, Belle's ex. I can focus on Blade."

"Sounds good to me."

Todd waved his hand. "I just had an idea, folks. I think we should use it to our advantage that you are both unknown in Deal. Both these gentlemen hang out at Toby's, our town's watering hole, for the majority of the day. Heck, you're way more likely to find them there than at their own homes, especially once noon rolls around. I say that Cosette goes into Toby's, sits at the bar and sees if one of the scoundrels approaches her. I'm betting at least one of them will. Town folks are nosy and they can spot a newcomer from miles away.

Say that you are my cousin's high school friend and you're in town visiting. I'll give her a heads up so she covers for us. To give you some background information, my cousin's name is Regina Caldwell. She grew up in Florida but has lived in Deal for the past ten years. She's a hairdresser, works in the next town over, Genoa. You're roughly the same age, so, it's believable. My cousin and I are cordial together but not very close, so, they'll be more likely to be loose lipped with you, if they connect you to Regina. Plus, they would clam up in a New York minute if they knew that you are law enforcement."

"I like that idea. I'll head on over there now."

Sheriff Booker turned to Tommy. "Why don't you lay low while Cosette goes to the bar."

"Will do. I can do some online research on Kurt and Blade."

6

Cosette walked down the main road to Toby's Bar. An all too familiar wave of nausea hit. *I'll order some ginger ale. Hopefully that'll help.*

Entering the establishment, Cosette's eyes struggled to adjust to the dimly lit room. Once in focus, she made her way over to the bar.

A pleasant looking, young woman with blazing red hair, thrown carelessly up into a top knot, was positioned behind the bar.

Her voice boomed out. "Hello there, stranger. You must be new in town?"

"Yeah, I'm just visiting."

"Well, welcome. What can I get ya?"

"A ginger ale, please."

The bartender giggled. "I sure don't get a lot of requests for pop drinks here. My clients tend to prefer the hard stuff."

"Too early in the day for that."

Cosette was aware that her pregnancy was not showing yet. For this particular assignment, masking her pregnancy was ideal.

A movement in the corner of the bar caught Cosette's attention. She glanced over and saw a man sitting alone in a booth, a book placed on the table in front of him was his only companion.

Their eyes met and his dimples deepened as he smiled at her. The classically handsome man sported a shock of dark chestnut, brown hair. She estimated that he was in his thirties.

Knowing that it was crucial to interact with the town's residents, once Cosette received her beverage, she meandered over to his booth.

"Hey, there."

The man was once again thoroughly engrossed in his book. He appeared startled by Cosette's sudden proximity to him.

"Well, hello. Looks like an interesting read."

"It is. I'm a bit of a mystery book addict."

"I can relate. I love reading too."

"I'm Blade...Blade Florence. Who do I have the honor of speaking with?"

"I'm Cosette."

"Beautiful name! Why don't you have a seat?"

"Don't mind if I do."
Cosette settled into the seat across from him.

"So, what brings you into our humble, little town?"

"I'm visiting a friend."

"Oh? Who? It's a small town. We all know each other."

"Regina Caldwell. We've been friends since high school. She's at work right now so I figured I'd have a look around. It's a charming town."

"Thank you. Kind of partial to it myself."

"Where are you from?"

Florida, born and raised."

"That's right. Regina grew up there. So nice that you're still friends after all these years."

"Yeah, Regina's a great girl. Such a loyal friend too."

"She's a very nice lady. Say, if you haven't gone yet, I'd recommend you eat at Hal's. They have the best darn pizza within a hundred mile radius. It's mind blowing how delicious it is."

"I'm starting to feel a little hungry. Might head on over there after I finish my drink."

"It's just a few doors down. I wouldn't mind getting a bite to eat myself. Mind if I join you?"

"That sounds nice, Blade. I'd love the company."

Once their glasses were empty. Blade and Cosette exited the bar and strolled to Hal's.

The heat of the day hit them like a slap across the face. The road resembled a smooth, black river. Waves of heat rose off the sun-drenched asphalt. Cosette could feel the warmth from the pavement penetrating through the bottom of her sandals.

Entering the restaurant felt like showering under a cool waterfall. The air conditioning was working overtime. Cosette sighed in relief.

Hal's was bustling. A fatigued looking hostess greeted them unenthusiastically.

"Hey folks, the wait is about twenty minutes for a table. There's a couple of spots at the bar available now, if you're interested."

Blade looked over at Cosette, raising his eye brow.

"The bar sounds just fine." Cosette responded.

"Okey doke...Here's a couple of menus. Head on over to the two vacant seats at the far left of the bar. Enjoy your lunch."

"I can see that this is a popular place. It's packed."

"Yup, always is."

Just then, Cosette noticed a memorial poster of Belle London. Pretending that she had no idea who the young lady was, Cosette stated, "Who's the girl on the memorial poster over there?"

"That's Belle London, a local high school student."

"She's so young. Why'd she pass away?"

"It's a horrible story. She was murdered!"

"Murdered? How tragic! Is the killer behind bars?"

"Not yet, unfortunately. We've had two murders in town recently."

"Could it be a serial killer? Two murders in such a small town seems pretty extreme to me."

"Who knows? Even Sheriff Booker seems to be pretty much clueless about it."

"Do you have any theories about who the killer or killers are?"

"Well, Belle had a crazy ex. He was pretty destroyed when she dumped him.

Rumor around town is that he was seriously stalking her. But, I doubt he would kill the other victim...a sweet, old lady from town."

"So, do you think there are two different killers, Blade?"

"I'm not sure. The sheriff is being tight lipped. His own family doesn't even know the details about the murders. Nobody even knows if they were killed in the same manner. Why don't we change the subject. This isn't the most pleasant lunch conversation."

Cosette questioned. "I'm surprised you feel that way since you love reading murder mysteries."

"Reading a make-believe story isn't the same as discussing two actual murders of people I've known my whole life."

Cosette sensed it was time to back off from her questioning. She didn't want Blade to grow suspicious of her.

"Of course, you're right. Now, let's have some pizza."

The remainder of the lunch was uneventful. Cosette normally had a sixth sense about people. So far, she did not pick up anything shady or questionable off of Blade. In fact, he remained a perfect gentleman with her and even insisted on paying for their meal. Cosette noticed that Blade signed the check with his left hand.

Hmm, he's a leftie. What are the odds? The killer is left handed too. I'll need to keep a close eye on him.

7

LATE SUMMER, DEAL, NEVADA

Winter and her mother had just finished their cucumber sandwiches when their doorbell rang. Winter sprang up and opened the door.

"Jenna! You're timing is impeccable. We just finished lunch. Come on in."

"Actually, I have a question. My stepmom, Quinn, and I are going to the mall. We'd love it if you'd join us. I know it's kind of last minute. Maybe you already have plans?"

"No, I don't. That sounds great. Let me grab my purse and we can be on our way. Can I meet you in five minutes?"

"Sure, we'll be in Quinn's car. Take your time, though. We aren't in any rush. She's about as chill as a person can get. I think you're really going to like her. It's long overdue that you meet each other. Can't believe you haven't crossed paths all summer."

"I agree! I've been wanting to meet her. I'll be right over."

Winter applied her favorite lipgloss, a shimmery raspberry tint and combed her hair. Peeking her head into her mother's office she exclaimed, "Mom, I'm going to the mall with Jenna and her stepmom. I'll be back soon."

"Ok, honey. Have fun."

Winter stepped outside into the oppressive heat. *Good thing it's an indoor mall since it's such a scorching day.*

Winter spotted Quinn's silver Escalade, walked over and hoisted herself up into the car from the running board.

"Winter, this is my stepmom, Quinn. Quinn, this is Winter. You finally get to meet."

An effervescent, warm lady with soulful, maple colored eyes and honey blonde hair pulled into a topknot, made Winter feel comfortable instantly.

"Winter, it's so wonderful to meet you! I've heard such amazing things about you from Jenna. How are you enjoying our town so far?"

"It's been great, Mrs. Booker."

"Please call me Quinn. When you call me Mrs. Booker, I can't help but look to see if you're talking to my mother in law."

The car exploded into laughter. Quinn's enthusiasm and upbeat mood was infectious. They blasted the music the entire way to the mall.

The trio shopped until they dropped. By the time Quinn went to her manicure appointment, Jenna and Winter were famished.

"Winter, I'm starving. Let's have dinner at Gia's Diner. It's on the lower level of the mall. The food is super good!"

"Yes, please! I'm so hungry that I'm starting to feel shaky."

The friends settled into a booth and immediately ordered lemonades.

"Your stepmom is incredible!"

"Isn't she? I won the lottery when my dad met her. She's even an English teacher at our high school. My friends all adore her too. She's pretty much the go-to person when anyone has problems. Actually, my friends confide in her even more than they confide in me."

"You're so lucky. May I ask where your biological mother is?"

"She died of an aneurism when I was only five years old. I remember her still but, sadly, the memories are gradually fading. My parents were crazy about each other. Dad never thought he'd be able to find love again but, then, Quinn came along and changed all that. She's brought so much laughter and happiness into our lives. Quinn's quite a bit younger than dad. Kind of glad she didn't have kids before she met him. All the focus is on me. She loves me as if I were her own kid. I hope we both end up in her class this school year. We find out our schedules tomorrow. Can you believe that school is starting in under a week? Where did the summer go?"

"Tell me about it! I'm super nervous about starting school here."

"I know it's easier said than done, but, try not to be nervous. After all, you already have a pretty big group of friends. My friends all adore you. Which reminds me, are you game for going to the barn tonight? Kind of our last hoorah of the summer."

"I'd love that."

"Great, as soon as Quinn's nail appointment is over, we can head home. I can drive us there at about 8:00?"

Just then, Quinn rushed up to their table and settled into the booth next to Jenna.

"Girls! Are you obsessed?"
Quinn flashed her flawless nails at them.

Winter was mesmerized by their vibrant red color and shine.

"Wow! Your nails are beautiful!"

"Thanks so much! I figured it would be nice to start off the school year with a new set of nails."

Quinn turned to Jenna. "Your dad and I have a date tonight. I'm so excited. He's been working around the clock because of those dreadful murders. I finally talked him into taking me to that new Italian bistro in Genoa."

"I've heard the food there is excellent, Mom. You deserve to be pampered. Dad has been basically radio silent since the murders. It'll be good for both of you to get out."

"I agree, sweet pea. If you girls are ready, I can take you home. No rush whatsoever though."

"Yes, we're ready, Mom."

Winter interjected. "Thanks so much, Quinn. I had the greatest time with you and Jenna. You both make me feel so welcome. It helps with my homesickness a lot."

The ladies whipped out of the mall parking lot and got onto the highway. Suddenly, Quinn abruptly stopped the car.

"Oh dear, girls...what's that crossing the road up ahead?"

Winter surveyed the road and to her horror saw a frightened cocker spaniel traversing the road. The animal was narrowly hit by a speeding car.

Quinn screamed out. "We need to help her!"

"Mom, it's so dangerous to stop here!"

"I'm sure as hell not going to let this puppy get injured. Over my dead body!"

Quinn screeched the car to a halt, hopped out of the vehicle and waved her hands in the air as a signal to approaching drivers.

In one graceful swoop, Quinn scooped up the puppy and brought her into the safety of their car.

Winter was in awe of what she had just witnessed. Of course, it was standard that anyone should come to the rescue of an animal, but Quinn went above and beyond. She put her own life at risk to save the scared, little puppy.

Winter had already liked Quinn a great deal before, but the bravery and selflessness she had just displayed, deepened Winter's adoration for her all the more.

8

Winter returned home from the night out with her friends shortly after midnight. Her mother, still working in her office, greeted her when she came through the front door.

"Honey, did you have a good time?"

"More than I can even begin to describe. I never thought I would say this, but I feel so included here already. Jenna and I are as thick as thieves and I also love her friend group. Correction, *our* friend group. They all make me feel so included. I still miss Jules, of course, and my other friends back home, but I'm truly happy here!"

"I can't tell you how relieved it makes me to hear you say that, honey. I love it here, too. In fact, I'm having coffee tomorrow morning with Quinn, Jenna's stepmom."

"You are? That's so cool. I think you two will really hit it off. She's a hoot and kind hearted to the core. By the way, why are you still up, Mom? It isn't like you. You're normally in bed by ten."

"I know...had to finish up a project. Feeling pretty tired. I'll head to bed now. Your dad crashed soon after he came home from work. He was beat. Don't stay up too much longer. It's late."

"I won't. Sweet dreams."

Winter headed to her bedroom. The full moon, a glowing, white orb loomed large, a cobra-black, desert sky served as its background. It was surrounded by the eerie glow of the moon, scattered clouds danced lazily around it. The moon cast so much light tonight, that Winter did not need to turn on the lamp in her room. She lowered herself onto her plush bed, fatigue pulling at her eyes.

Winter loved to keep her window cracked at night and listen to the sounds of the neighboring forest's nocturnal wildlife. A lone owl hooted. She was beginning to drift off when a sound in the distance interrupted her impending sleep.

Tip toeing to the window, Winter strained to listen. All was silent for a moment. Then, the sound started again. She could hear people speaking in the distance. It didn't sound like normal, everyday conversation, more like rhythmic chants.

Fear crept along Winter's spine. *What's that sound? It sounds like people in the forest behind our house. I'm starting to know these woods pretty well. I should have a peek and see what's going on. Maybe there's a party I don't know about.*

Noiselessly slipping out of the back, sliding glass door, Winter moved through her backyard and into the undergrowth of the forest. She startled when she felt a whoosh in front of her face. A hungry owl flew out of the inky sky and swooped down onto a skittering rat, her talons impaling and instantly killing the poor creature. Winter took deep breaths in order to try to calm her frayed nerves.

It's just an owl. No big deal. He obviously needs to eat too. The noise I heard from my room was not wildlife. It sounded human.

Winter continued to plod through the forest. Her clammy skin was covered with goosebumps.

After a few minutes, she reached a clearing in the forest. A light flickered in the distance. Feeling confident that nobody was around, Winter crept over to the mysterious light. There was a candle positioned on top of an old tree stump.

This is so weird. Somebody was obviously just here. Who is lighting candles in a forest in the middle of the night? I need to get back home. I've seen enough.

Winter started to make a bee-line for her home. The forest was eerily quiet. Suddenly, she detected footsteps rapidly approaching her. She quickened her pace.

What have I gotten myself into? I should have stayed in the safety of my own house!

Winter felt a strong hand grasping her shoulder. Screaming out in sheer terror, she turned to face the menacing figure. A large man, several years older than her, looked at her inquisitively.

"What are you doing out here in the middle of the night, little lady?"

"Who are you?"

"I'm Blade. Who are you? I know everyone in Deal but I don't recognize you."

"I'm Winter Wells...Just moved here at the beginning of summer. Why are you here at this time of night?"

"I work the late shift at the gas station on the other side of town. This is the short cut I take to get home. I'll ask again. What is a young lady like you doing alone here?"

"I heard these weird noises from my bedroom window...Figured I'd go and inspect."

"Noises? What kind of noises?"

"Like people chanting. It went on for a few minutes...very rhythmical. Then, I came out here and found a burning candle over on a tree stump. Why on earth would someone light a candle here?"

"Who knows? Maybe an amorous couple had a late-night picnic. Listen, I have no idea what you heard but I strongly advise you from wandering around alone, especially at this hour. You may not be aware that there have been two murders in Deal recently. The killer is still on the loose."

"I do know and I was dumb to venture out here."

"You said it, not me." Blade chuckled.

"Let me walk you home."

"Thanks, Sir."

"Sir? You make it sound like I'm eighty years old. Call me Blade."

"Blade, it is."

Winter let out a huge sigh of relief when she was once again safely cocooned in her bedroom. She was grateful for Blade's kindness and chivalry.

This night could have ended so much worse than it did. Thank goodness for Blade. He was like my knight in shining armor...and he sure is handsome. Little too old for me, Mom and Dad would freak out. That would be half the fun!

After a few minutes of laying on her bed, Winter felt restless and headed over to her window. What she saw startled her. Blade was standing statue-still between the trees in her backyard. His eyes appeared to be transfixed on Winter's bedroom window. She stood motionless, goosebumps erupted on her skin. Slowly, she stepped away from the window, attempting to remain undetected, and crawled under the safety of her covers.

Twenty minutes later, she summoned the courage to peer back out of her window. To Winter's horror, Blade was still standing in the same spot. He appeared zombie like.

9

DEEP IN THE FOREST, DEAL, NEVADA

"You'd better have a damn good reason for asking me to meet you here in the middle of the night! I was fast asleep."

"I do! I swear! Please, hear me out." He cowered before the demon-like figure.

"Go ahead, I'm waiting."

"I'm in some major hot water with Abbott because I massacred that old bag, Mrs. Brownson. You directed me to kill her but now I'm taking the heat. Abbott even beat the hell out of me because he was so pissed off."

"And, I care that you're in trouble because…?"

"I told Abbott that you directed me to commit the murders of both Belle and Ruth Brownson. He questioned that you are the divine leader. Abbott insisted that he's in charge and that I shouldn't be taking any direction from you. The rest of the cult members know that you're the lead but apparently Abbott hasn't gotten the memo yet."

The demon's face split into an evil sneer.

"Let me make one thing crystal clear. You are to follow my instructions and only my instructions. I don't care what Abbott thinks. I'll cut him into tiny pieces if he ever undermines my authority again. And, if you don't bow to my every command, you'll be found mutilated in a chicken coop yourself. Got it?"

"Of course! Please, forgive me. I know that you're the one and only leader."

"I should hope so! I have an assignment for you. There's another pesky high school girl I need you to get rid of."

"Oh no, a high school girl again? This town is already so freaked out because of pretty, little Belle's murder."

"Are you going to listen to my commands or not?"

"Of course, I am! Please give me the details and she will be eliminated..."

TWO MONTHS EARLIER
BELLE LONDON

"Belle, are you seriously going to meet a complete stranger on the football field tonight?"

"Shh, quiet down, Lis! My mom is going to end up overhearing us."

"Sorry, you're right. Discretion has never been one of my strong suits. I'll whisper."

"And...yes, I'm meeting him. So excited. It's about time. Not like we're rushing into anything. We've been talking on Snapchat for a couple months already."

"I know, Belle, and I get why you're tempted but I keep hearing about cat-fishing on the news. Meeting a complete stranger is just plain risky! For all you know, Jeremy isn't actually who he says he is. You've never even face-timed him. Just promise me that you'll be careful?"

"You can be such a nervous Nilly. Of course, I promise. We both know I have plenty of experience with the opposite sex. Something tells me I'll be able to handle myself just fine. I'm thinking of wearing my cropped red shirt and denim shorts. Do you think that looks great on me?"

"Are you kidding? To die for, but, then again, you could wear a burlap sack and still look like a top model."

"Thanks! Flattery will get you everywhere."

"You know it's true…So, what time is the meet up?"

"We said we'd meet at 11:00. Figured that'll allow plenty of time for everyone to clear out after the football game."

"Ok, I'm excited for you but please, at least, text me as soon as your date with him is over."

"Obviously, Lis. I'll fill you in on all the juicy details. I get the feeling that this could be the start of something hot and heavy."

Belle had a difficult time concentrating on the football game.

In just a few short hours, I'll finally be in Jeremy's arms. It's about time. I've been very patient.

After the game ended, Belle went with her army of friends to Hal's. Lis, her best friend, was the only one who was aware of her date.

Normally, I love being the center of attention but tonight I could do without it. It won't be the easiest task to slip away unnoticed from the gang.

Aaron, one of Belle's closest friends, snapped his fingers in the air.

"Earth to Belle. Are you ok? You seem pre-occupied tonight and you've barely had a bite of your pizza."

"I've been better. My stomach feels a little off. What time is it anyway?"

He glanced at his phone. "It's 10:38."

Belle stated, "I should probably get going. I just don't feel great. I need to get some sleep."

Aaron raised an eyebrow. "I'll walk you home."

"Don't be silly. My house is a two minute walk away. I'll be home in no time. Stay here and hang out still."

"Are you sure?"

"Positive! I'll see you tomorrow."

Belle bid her friends farewell and darted out of the restaurant, feeling relieved that she was able to get away without too much of an argument from them. Nothing could foil her plans for tonight.

Plodding up the hill to the high school, excitement enveloped her. This was the moment of truth. She was about to meet her crush.

The floodlights from the game had long been extinguished. The full moon and a single, dimly lit streetlight were her only sources of light.

Bats encircled the light. They darted and turned sharply into the swarm of moths.

Belle always knew that she was a bit of a daredevil. She had been this way her entire life. She could still remember when her parents took the training wheels off of her bike.

They took her to a nearby elementary school playground.
Three children from her class were also there learning to ride a bike that day. The other kids squealed and clung to their parents, scared out of their minds.
Belle, on the other hand, raced away and crashed straight into a nearby wall, never flinching for a minute. She was gutsy. Her family told her she was simply wired to be that way.

Belle didn't think she was being very brave at the moment. She felt chills dance across her spine. This location was isolated. Other than bats, she was completely on her own. Alone was not something she was accustomed to being.

Belle counted her blessings that she had always been popular and surrounded by adoring friends. She knew she was the 'it girl' although she would never admit that to anyone. Being modest and kind was part of her charm.

She looked out over the darkened field…sheer emptiness.

I'm being silly. I've been on this field hundreds of times. Jeremy will be here before I know it and then I will have a magical night. Dad always says that you miss 100% of the shots you don't take. I trust my instincts. I really like this boy. Plus, he lives miles away. Pretty nice that he's even going out of his way to come to my hometown. I just need to chill. I'm a little early…it'll give me time to lay out the picnic blanket, light candles and pour the champagne.

That is just what Belle did. By the time she completed her set up, she took a step back and appraised the scene she had created.

This is impressive. It looks like those fantasy date scenes the producers create on reality dating shows. If this doesn't encourage romance, I'm not sure what will. Now, I just need to sit down and wait for Jeremy to get here.

Giving her silky, long locks a final combing, she delicately laid back on the padded, picnic blanket.

The night sky had always been a peaceful sight for Belle. As a child, her parents would often lay out a blanket at night in the backyard by the swimming pool. Her family would have ice-cream sundaes and stare at the universe above them.

Belle prided herself on being able to easily identify the phases of the moon,various constellations such as Orion and even the red, flaming ball of Mars.

Tonight, the heavens were teeming with twinkling stars. They were familiar friends to her and they seemed to be supporting her with this all-important meeting with Jeremy. The stars had been a source of calm to her, like a quiet, non-judging friend.

Appearing as a sign of love and comfort from the heavens, a perfectly divine glow of light shimmered through the sky. It was a shooting star! Belle quickly made a wish as she watched it tango and finally plummet from the pitch darkness.

Please let tonight be everything I've ever dreamed of. Make Jeremy, the man of my dreams, become a reality.

Just then, Belle heard a rustling from the nearby bushes.

"Jeremy, is that you?" She giggled flirtatiously. There was no response.

"Oh, Jeremy, I've been waiting for you. Show yourself. I can't wait to get our night started. This champagne isn't going to drink itself."

A large figure emerged from the underbrush. Belle's pulse quickened and she thought. *Well, he certainly has the same body as in the photos he sent me. What a hunk. I'm officially in love.*

"Jeremy, I'm so excited to meet you. I feel like I've been waiting for our meeting for a lifetime.

There was complete silence as he approached.

"Jeremy? Are you ok?"

"I'm more than ok, baby. You're even more beautiful in real life than you are in your photos."

"And, you're just as charming as you are in our Snapchat messages. Come on over here. I want to get a better look at you."

The beast-like figure moved out of the shadows and closer to Belle. In the darkness, she could see something glinting. Just then, he raised his arms up. She saw the ax seconds before the sharp edge landed on her forehead. Then, her entire world went black.

10

**PRESENT DAY
RENO, NEVADA, POLICE
DEPARTMENT**

Frank entered the conference room with a stern look on his face.

"Tommy, Cosette, I'm eager to hear what you found out while you were in Deal."

Tommy chimed in first. "Wish I could tell you that we have a person of interest. Sheriff Booker gave us the name of two gentlemen to keep an eye out for. I interviewed one of them, an ex of Belle London, Kurt. I'm just not convinced that he's our guy. For starters, he has an airtight alibi. He was at a bar that night and cameras at the establishment clearly show him there during the hours of Belle's murder and even way beyond. Now, this is just my instinct, but, I kind of think he's harmless...Just a heartbroken, love-sick man. Cosette can tell you about what she thought of Blade Florence."

"Yes, Blade was an interesting character. I met him at the local bar in Deal. After drinks, we went over to the pizza parlor for lunch. Believe me, I'm far from eliminating him as a person of interest but based off of what I saw, he didn't seem off in any way. Call it a sixth sense, but I don't think he's connected to the murders. Now, that's not to say that he's off the hook, of course. Those are just my preliminary thoughts."

Frank surveyed Cosette and Tommy's notes. "Ok, well you both took very thorough notes. Good job! I appreciate that. For novice detectives, you're both doing an outstanding job. Heck, for experienced detectives, you're doing great! I spoke with the sheriff. He's equally impressed with you and would like you both to go back to Deal. Since Belle London was a high school student, he was hoping that one of you could go undercover at Deal High. Now, I know it sounds like a daunting task to act like an eighteen year old but I truly believe it can be done. Cosette, you still look like a teen and if we dress you a certain way, your pregnancy will not show for a couple more months still. By then, I have a feeling this case will be cracked wide open."

"I'm happy to go undercover as a high school student if it saves lives and catches the killer. What's the plan, Frank?"

"The Reno PD has rented a quaint, little home on the outskirts of Deal. Our story will be that Cosette's parents recently died in a car accident and your uncle is now taking custody of you. Tommy will be your uncle. You'll be enrolled in Deal High as a senior. The school starts up after summer break in a handful of days from now. That gives us a little time to get our ducks in a row. Tommy, Cosette, this is a pretty intense assignment. Are you both up for it?"

In unison, the duo responded, "I am!"

Frank continued. "And, in case you're wondering, I get that Blade has already seen you, Cosette. He doesn't have kids so he probably won't be around the high school. My advice to you, Cosette, is stay out of the bar where you met him. Sheriff told me that he pretty much sticks to his house, his job at the gas station or that bar. There's no reason for Blade to bump into you otherwise. Tommy can do the food shopping in town, or better yet, have the groceries delivered to your place. Cosette, you can throw on a baseball cap and sunglasses when you are out and about in town. Blade will never notice you. To be extra sure that he doesn't recognize you, it wouldn't hurt if you did a dramatic color change to your hair like platinum blonde or jet black. Tommy will keep a pretty low profile so that Kurt, Belle's ex doesn't see him. He isn't in high school anyway. So, just like Blade, you won't really bump into him if you stay away from that bar. I'd like you to move in to your new home in the next couple days, get situated. I believe that if Cosette can get close to some of Belle's friends, we may be able to solve this case before more people die. Her friends were pretty tight lipped when they were interviewed by the cops. Her best friend admitted that Belle was going to meet a suitor the night she was killed...a boy she had been communicating with on the app, Snapchat. Problem is, on that app, messages delete soon after they are seen. There's no way for us to track who she was messaging. That's where you come in, Cosette. They may be more loose lipped if you become a trusted friend."

11

Cosette had exactly one hour before Luke got home from work. She went onto their sprawling pool deck, lit candles and turned on the outside heaters. Even though the days were incredibly hot, the desert cooled off a great deal once the sun set.

She had prepared one of Luke's favorite meals, fettuccine with scallops. Tonight needed to be extra special. She was leaving for Deal the following day and wanted to make their night together magical.

Cosette didn't think it was possible but she had fallen even more deeply in love with her fiancé.

She had met him on a flight when she worked as a flight attendant. She was mesmerized with him from the moment he entered the aircraft. Since Cosette was still married at the time, albeit in a loveless marriage, they were friends at first. Once her cold, demeaning husband, Chad, had filed for divorce, Cosette pursued a relationship with Luke.

They both fell head over heels in love with each other. He proposed to her months later. Unexpectedly, Cosette discovered that she was pregnant a couple of months ago. Although, they had not planned to add a child to their family quite yet, both were overjoyed with the news.

Spencer, Cosette's son from her first marriage, was elated by the upcoming birth as well. As a family, they had decided not to discover the gender of the baby before birth because they enjoyed the anticipation.

"Cosette, I'm home."

"Out back, sweetie pie."

The love of her life meandered into their sprawling backyard. Their beloved Rhodesian Ridgeback, Trixie, and Romeo, their roadrunner, came bounding down to her as well. She couldn't help but laugh. What a sight for sore eyes they all were.

Romeo had been a regular visitor at Cosette's cottage in Virginia City. She had grown very attached to him. Sadly, he had injured himself and a local veterinarian felt it would be best for him not to be released back into the desert. Luke and Cosette had gladly adopted him. He had become a treasured member of their family. In fact, he was even featured among the photos in their last Christmas card.

"Sweetheart, I've been waiting to see you all day. Can't believe you're going to Deal in two days. I'm going to miss you so much."

"I'll miss you too. My goal is to solve this case stat and get back to you, Spencer and our family."

"I love the sound of that, sweetheart."

"I made your favorite, fettuccine with scallops."

"I thought that was the aroma I was picking up on. I'm starving. It's been a long day. One of my servers quit and the bar was packed. It was super stressful."

"Sorry to hear that. I guarantee you this meal will make you feel much better. Spencer gets home in an hour. He'll love it too."

The couple sat down for their sumptuous meal.

"I can't tell you how proud I am of you, Cosette. You were determined to make a difference after your best friend, Maggie's, senseless murder. Not only did you go to the police academy but you got hired on as a homicide detective and now you've been thriving in your new career."

"Your support and love mean the world to me."

Luke continued. "That being said, I wanted to talk to you before you left for Deal."

His brow furrowed.

"I know you're highly skilled at your job. I've no doubt about that, but, I can't help but feel a little nervous. I need you to be extra safe, sweetheart. Working undercover as a high school student can't be easy. Promise me that you'll take every precaution. I would die if you or our baby ever got hurt. Please!"

"Of course, I'm dedicated to my job, but, naturally, our family is most important to me. I'd never put any of us in jeopardy.

You have my word. If I ever feel that I've gotten in over my head, I'll come home. I can assure you of that 100%."

12

The following morning, Cosette headed to the shopping mall in Reno.

After some online research of the latest styles for teenage girls, she felt updated enough to know what sort of clothes to buy so she would blend in at Deal High School.

Having to hide her somewhat bloated abdomen, made the task even more daunting. Cosette spent hours going from store to store. She had bags full of cut off jean shorts, sweater vests, colorful cardigans, patterned jeans, Converse High-Tops and chunky platform sandals.

After leaving the mall, she went to Amber, her hair stylist, armed with photos from Teen Vogue and CosmoGirl. Her beautician cut stylish curtain bangs, trimmed a few inches off of her ends and dyed her locks a striking, icy blonde.

When presented with the results, Cosette was in awe of how her hair looked. It was the latest, cutting-edge style. She looked even more youthful than usual...young enough to pass as a high school senior.

Her hair stylist gasped. "I love your natural, chestnut hair, but, you're sure stunning as a blonde too. You're the spitting image of Marilyn Monroe!"

"I've never gone this blonde. The lightest I've ever been is a honey streaked brown but I love this. As usual, you did an amazing job. You're a magician!"

"Thanks, but, you're the ideal palette to work on, Not much doesn't look great on you!"

As Cosette was exiting the hair salon, her phone rang.

"Hi Tommy! Guess what I just did?"

"I'm intrigued. What?"

"I just transformed into a blonde! I'm surprised how much I love the look. I've always been partial to being a brunette. Also, before my hair appointment, I went to the mall and stocked up on a bunch of high school, age-appropriate clothes. Still have some packing to do tonight but I'll be all ready for us to head down to Deal tomorrow morning. That'll give us a couple days to get situated in our new home before Deal High starts."

"You're on top of things. I have a feeling the majority of my time down in Deal will be dedicated to fending off the young men from you! I'm pretty much ready to head out too. Just have a couple things still to do. Shall I pick you up at about nine?"

"Nine works for me. That'll give me time to see Spencer off to school before we leave."

"Great and I think we'll be fine down there with just my car. I figure the high school is within walking distance to our place. If you need the car in the evenings, you can have it. The majority of my days will consist of hunkering down in our house and doing online searches and other work. If for some reason, we feel it is too difficult for us to share one car, we can always get yours next weekend. Do you agree?"

"Absolutely, I think one car will be enough. See you tomorrow morning."

Cosette pulled into her driveway. The exhaustion from the day was beginning to pull at her. Luke was mesmerized by her new hair.

"Sweetheart, you look ravishing, as always!"

"You know how to make me feel special. That's one of the million reasons why I love you so much! I can hardly wait for our wedding day. We'll be husband and wife in just some months from now."

"I'm counting the minutes. I can't wait for our baby to arrive and for you to become my wife. We'll be a family of four not including our beloved pets."

Luke ordered Thai take-out and the family enjoyed a relaxing evening at home. By 8:00, Cosette could barely keep her eyes open. She stretched out on their bed and was asleep moments later.

SIX WEEKS EARLIER
RUTH BROWNSON

Ruth had just celebrated her seventy-eighth birthday with her family. It was a get-together she would not soon forget. She shared five children with the love of her life and husband of fifty-three years, Stuart.

The couple had been blessed with three girls and two boys.

Ruth's sisters would always joke that she had the ability to get pregnant if a strong wind blew in her direction. She thanked God that fertility issues were never a problem she had to deal with. All five pregnancies and births were equally trouble-free and seamless.

Their children lived in other parts of Nevada now. Shelly, their youngest, lived the closest to them, in Reno.

Ruth was not aware that her husband had already been planning a surprise party for her birthday for several months. Stuart had arranged for all of their children, grandchildren and Ruth's treasured sisters to come to their home.

He had sent Ruth to the supermarket, feigning that they were out of bread. By the time she returned, their home was filled with loved ones. Ruth, not one to cry easily, teared up from sheer joy. What a celebration it had been!

Ruth woke up the following morning, bright and early. Every bedroom in their spacious, ranch home was full to capacity with family. She wanted to make ham and mushroom omelets for her guests.

She looked over and saw that Stuart was just beginning to awaken.

"Stuart, dear, I'm going to go to the chicken coop and collect the eggs. You know how much our kids love my famous ham omelets."

"Darling, I want you to rest still. Let me collect the eggs and make breakfast."

"Now, that's just nonsense…you know how much I love cooking for our family. Go on back to sleep. It's way too early for you to be awake already."

The conversation was interrupted by their rambunctious rooster, Howie. He called out to alert them that morning had finally arrived.

Ruth exited their home quietly and slipped into the backyard. She crossed the dew-filled meadow. The rising sun cast a pinkish hue. Golden fingers of sunlight caressed the morning sky. The air was fresh and a soft wind brushed against Ruth's weary face, giving her a much needed boost of energy.

The dawn chorus of birds chirping drifted across the property. The crystal-blue sky was dotted with white, ghost-like clouds.

Stuart had repurposed the playhouse into a chicken coop once their children had gone off to college. It was an impressive coop and it had even won awards for its unique design.

It consisted of ten nesting boxes and an entry and exit ramp into the playhouse. It was the ideal set-up because Ruth's treasured chickens could decide if they preferred to stay in the confines of the indoor space or exercise in the enclosed garden connected to the structure.

Ruth entered the chicken coop and retrieved her straw padded basket. Her favorite chicken, Betty, ran to her. The affectionate bird rubbed her beak against Ruth's ankles and attempted to preen her.

"Good morning, my sweet Betty. Did you sleep well, my love? Where are the rest of your sisters? Your mommy needs to make some wonderful omelets this morning. I hope my girls delivered."

Betty dutifully followed Ruth as she approached the playhouse. The warm-hearted, elderly lady pried the door open. She was met with the usual gloomy darkness. As her eyes adjusted to the darkness, Ruth saw her pets calmly roosting.

Off in the corner, she spotted a darkened figure. The demon shadow emerged and approached her at a rapid speed. Before she had a chance to scream, a shiny object glinted above her. An ax bore down. Pain seared in her head and time froze. Her entire life replayed in fast forward. She could hear her cherished rooster crow. Then, Ruth's world went black.

PRESENT DAY
COSETTE AND TOMMY'S
MOVING DAY TO DEAL

Tommy arrived bright and early the following morning.

"Your chariot awaits, Madame."

"Thank you, Tommy, or should I say *Uncle Phil*? After all, that will be your temporary identity while we are in Deal. We had better get used to our pseudonyms."

"I agree, *Indigo Clemson.* Shucks, that name's gonna take some getting used. Who comes up with these names?"

"In this case, your dad picked the names." Cosette giggled and continued. "Indigo is a unique name but I think it's pretty…Sounds sort of edgy to me."

"You're right! It does have a ring to it. Shall we head out,…Indigo?"

"You bet,…Uncle."

The duo headed to Deal. The drive went by in a flash. Before they knew it, the GPS was giving its final directions.

Cosette pointed. "I bet it's that cottage coming up." She strained to see the numbers on the mailbox. Once she was able to identify the address, she declared, "Yup, that's it. How adorable!"

Tommy pulled into the long, gravel driveway. "Home sweet home. I like it! Let's go look inside."

The cottage stood in a grove of White Fir trees. It had a warm and inviting feel to it.

Once inside, Tommy and Cosette toured the home. The walls were sturdy and had wooden planks painted in a traditional white.

A wine rack and a storage cabinet were tucked underneath the stairs. Wide, pine boards boasted their natural, golden grain.

Tommy was pleased with what he saw. "I love the different nooks of the cottage. It's only two bedrooms and two baths but it still feels open and airy. Let's have a peek out back."

French doors opened to the back deck. Beyond that, was the sprawling wilderness.

"Look at the pond, Tommy! There's a turtle sunning on the edge."

"That's a Western Pond Turtle. I'd recognize them anywhere. I had one as a kid."

"What a cutie! I get this is a work assignment for us, but this adorable cottage definitely helps me feel at home."

LAST DAY OF SUMMER VACATION

"Winter, breakfast is ready!"

"It smells good, Mom. Your french toast is the best. Can't believe today is the last day before school starts. Where did the summer go?"

"It did go by unusually fast. Part of that's because we were so busy with moving…made time fly. What are you doing for your last day of vacation?"

"Quinn is taking Jenna and me to Lake Tahoe for the day. We'll hang out at the beach and have a picnic. I've never been there. Heard it's a gorgeous place."

"I went there a handful of times when I studied at Berkeley. It's breathtaking."

"I can't wait and I'm so excited that Quinn is my teacher for first period. She's the coolest!"

"Yeah, you really lucked out. I bet your senior year will be great. I've been meaning to ask you, is Jules visiting us during Thanksgiving break?"

"Yeah, she called me last night. It's confirmed. She'll be here with us for Thanksgiving. I'm literally going to count down the days. Such a relief that her parents agreed."

13

A ghostly white, full moon loomed large in the clear night sky. Millions of stars were sprinkled about. Abbott gazed upon the celestial grandeur and was convinced that it elevated him to a higher universe

The galaxy is speaking to me. It sees me as the sole ruler of the universe. I just need to get the others to see that. This meeting will be crucial. I won't allow anyone to disrespect me or our mission.

The members slithered into the grove of trees. Their skin looked death-like due to the milky glow from the moon.

Once they were dutifully assembled in the forest clearing, Abbott stood tall behind the altar, full of self confidence and malice.

"Listen up, obviously you're all aware that school's about to start up. Soon after that, the Halloween season will arrive...our busy season. We need to make the most of this time. I want us to meet here at the next full moon. This will be a very special ceremony. We need to sacrifice a girl of high school age shortly before our next meeting. Her death will wield us incredible power...and, the follower who slays her, will receive great rewards. Do I make my assignment perfectly clear?"

The followers stared at Abbott in a trance-like state. With dilated pupils, they nodded and descended into the underbrush.

FIRST DAY OF SCHOOL-DEAL HIGH

Winter did an appraising glance in her full length mirror one last time. It was her first day of school. She stepped out into the blinding sunshine and proceeded on her five minute walk to Deal High. Heavy footsteps approached.

"Hey, Winter!"

"Zach! So nice to see you. Isn't this way out of the way from your house?"

Zach's cheeks reddened. "It is but I was eager to walk you on your first day of school. Zarina and Jenna wanted to be here for you but they had a student council meeting to get to before school. They told me to tell you that they'll see you in first period, Quinn's class."

You're so sweet to walk with me. Thanks. It certainly helps with my first day jitters."

"Hey, do you have any plans after school?"

"Not yet, why?"

"I was hoping we could go to Genoa and see a movie. Figure we won't have much homework yet since it's the first day of school."

"That sounds great. Will Jenna and the others come to the movie too?"

"Uh, I was kind of thinking that it would be just you and me."

"Oh, I'd like that."

Now, it was Winter's turn to blush. She had been harboring feelings for Zach ever since she had moved to Deal. Going on a date with him was a dream come true.

"Great, pick you up at 4:00?"

"Yeah, I'll be ready."

Winter and Zach arrived at school. They were both in Quinn's class for first period.

Winter selected a desk near the front of the classroom and Zach plopped down next to her. Quinn's entire face lit up when she saw them.

"Winter, Zach! Can I just say how elated I am that you two are in my class? We're going to have a great school year together."

Winter beamed in admiration. "We're the lucky ones. It's awesome that Jenna and Zarina are in this class too!"

"I'll say. You've all spent so much time together this summer. The class will basically be a continuation of that."

Cosette was running behind this morning, which was unlike her. She woke up feeling nauseous. Tommy gave her a bland, stomach-friendly breakfast. Once her queasiness had subsided, she made the trek to the high school. She had a pocket full of mints in case the nausea returned. Scanning her schedule, she quickly located the room for her first period, English 4 with Ms. Booker. Cosette was aware that this was Sheriff Booker's wife.

Her undercover work at the high school was top secret. Booker's wife was not even privy to it.

Jenna and Zarina sauntered in and took a seat near Winter.

Cosette entered the classroom next, a lump formed in her throat. She took a seat and pulled her purple notebook out. Her notebooks were color coordinated based on the subjects.

From the corner of her eye, Cosette noticed someone staring at her. She glanced over.

"Hi, I'm Winter. I just moved to town. It's my first day at this high school."

"Hey there, my name is Indigo. It's actually my first day at this high school too."

"Wow, we are both the new girls. It's nice to meet you. I moved to Deal at the beginning of the summer. I haven't seen you around town. Did you just move here?"

"Yeah, I actually moved here in the past week."

"Shoot, you sure didn't get a lot of time to settle in. I have a great group of friends here already. I'd love it if you hung out with us at lunch."

"That would be great. Thank you!"

"Sure, we'll hang out on the senior lawn. It's back behind the multi-use auditorium."

"I'll be there. Thanks, again."

Quinn commenced the class moments later. The hour flew by in a flash. Grammar and poetry had never been so fascinating for Winter. Quinn's teaching style was dynamic and patient. She captured everyone's attention with her jokes and relatable stories.

14

The bell rang to signal the start of lunch. Cosette located the senior lawn. A group of students had already assembled.

"Indigo, over here!" Winter motioned for her to sit on the bench next to her.

"Indigo, how have your classes been so far?"

"I really like them and everyone's been so nice."

"That's great! I've been loving it too. Let me introduce you to my friends. This is Jenna, Zach and Zarina."

The friendly students greeted her in unison.

Zarina, a beautiful, dark haired girl with sculpted cheekbones and a welcoming, broad smile, spoke first.

"Indigo, what brings you to Deal?"
Cosette felt her pulse quicken. She had been heavily rehearsing her story with Tommy.

"My parents were killed in a car accident."

The group gasped in sympathy. Zarina continued, "Oh my! I'm so sorry. Don't know what to say."

"Thanks. It's been like an endless nightmare. I moved here with my uncle. He's been great...not sure what I'd do without him."

Jenna continued. "My mom passed away years ago. If you ever need anyone to talk to, I'm here."

"I'm sorry to hear that, Jenna."

"It sucks but you know our teacher from first period? She married my dad years ago. She's basically my mom. Dad and I are lucky to have her."

Zarinna interrupted. "Guys, who wants to come with me to get a corn dog?"

The entire group stood up so they could escort Zarina. It was clear to Cosette that she was the leader of this group of friends. It was also obvious to her that this group was seen as the in-group of the school. Cosette may not have been in high school for several years now but she could still spot the tell-tale signs of the popular *crowd.* Everywhere they went on campus, they commanded respect. Each one wore the latest designer brands and walked with an air of confidence.

I have a feeling that this group of friends could end up being an invaluable resource about the murders in town. They seem well connected.

At four o'clock on the dot, Zach rang on Winter's door. She had a meadow of butterflies in her stomach.

"Hey, baby. Ready to go to the movies?"

"I sure am. I've heard it's a suspenseful film.

"I've heard the same. Dying to see it!"

Zach entwined his arm into Winter's and they were off.

After selecting their seats at the theater, Zach went to buy bottomless popcorn and drinks. Winter was beginning to relax. She reasoned to herself that they had been friends for months already. There was no reason to be anxious.

During the film, Zach did the classic date maneuver. He stretched and yawned. Then, his arm conveniently draped over Winter's shoulder. She eased into his embrace.

The movie had a series of suspenseful scenes. It was the perfect excuse for Winter to huddle in closer to

Zach. At the end of the evening, Zach drove her home.

"This was nice, baby. I'd love to do it again. Are you planning on going to the 'back to school' dance this weekend?"

"Yeah, I actually was planning on going."

Zach's dimples deepened. "I'd love it if you'd be my date?"

"That sounds great!"

He pulled curbside in front of Winter's house. Silence hung heavy in the air. Winter held her breath. She had been hoping that he would give her a goodnight kiss throughout the evening.

Just then, Zach slowly approached her. This was Winter's cue. She met him half way and they shared a soft, lingering kiss.

The evening had been perfect from start to finish.

15

Cosette fell asleep the moment she got home from school. By the time she woke back up, the sky was ablaze with the setting sun. Hues of pink and lavender illuminated Cosette's room.

She could smell the inviting aroma of freshly baked cookies. Stretching her arms skyward, Cosette pulled herself out of bed and went to look for Tommy.

She found him hunched over his laptop in the family room.

"Hi there, sleepy head. Did you rest well?"

"I crashed the minute my head hit the pillow. My energy level is so low. I can barely make it through the school day. I definitely had more energy when I was in high school last time."

"Well, you weren't pregnant then. I'm glad you slept. Made you some cookies. Let me get you a plate."

"You spoil me so much."

"That's my job. You're my best friend. I love pampering you."

Tommy handed Cosette the plate of still warm, gooey cookies and sat down next to her.

"Have I got things I need to tell you. I've been digging online all day... specifically the dark web."

"I'm all ears."

"Geez, I saw some haunting images today. I saw photos of both our victims after they were deceased."

"Are you serious?"

"Yup, they're all over the dark web. But, there's more. There's all kind of chatter online about cult activity in Deal."

"Wow! If that's true, then we're dealing with something much bigger than a single killer."

"Exactly…I'm starting to think that this cute, little town is pure evil and has lots of secrets. I contacted Debbie Wright. She's a local expert on the occult. In fact, Debbie has worked with our police department before. She's as knowledgeable as they get. Told her I'd swing by and see her tomorrow morning."

"Great news. In the meantime, I'll continue to be our eyes and ears at the high school. The back to school dance is this weekend. I'll be sure to go. If there are any after-parties, I'll be there too. Teens, especially, tend to get loose lipped when they're drinking."

Tommy set off bright and early the following morning to meet with Debbie Wright. Her office was located mid-point between Reno and Deal. He parallel parked in front of her office and darted into the building. Tommy pulled his scarf closer around his neck as an icy gust of wind blew. It was an unseasonably cold day

Nursing his coffee, Tommy knocked on Debbie's office door. A lady with a wide smile and a cherub-like face swung the door open.

"You must be Tommy?"

"Yes, I am. You're Debbie...I presume?"

"Yes, Sir. Come on in. It's so nice to meet you. I've been reading up on the murders in Deal ever since you reached out to me. I'm eager to discuss them with you."

"I am too. My dad told me what a wealth of information you are about cults. I was on the dark web yesterday and saw mentions of a cult in the Deal area. That caught my attention."

Debbie rubbed her temple as if she were fighting off a headache and continued.

"Yeah, there've been clear signs that there's cult activity in Deal or, at the very least, in the immediate vicinity. For starters, as you know, the dark web hints of nefarious cult activity in Deal. I'm able to monitor what is said there but who posts the information is untraceable. Around the time of Belle's death, someone on the dark web described being in a cult and that her death was connected to the group. Also, residents have reported finding candles and makeshift altars in the woods of Deal. Law enforcement has kept an eye on the area but they have yet to actually catch a group meeting there."

"Can you tell me more facts about cults?"

"Of course, a cult is a group of people with a particular fanatical and often dangerous ideology. Usually, there's one leader and he or she is worshipped by the other members. The leader tends to be manipulative and charismatic. Often, the members consider the lead to be a genius or superior in some other way. Leaders punish the members if they don't comply with the strict rules."

"So, if the leader wanted someone killed, the members would probably proceed and commit murder?"

"You better believe it. What the leader says is everything. Sleep deprivation and drugs are commonly used to break down the members' defenses. These methods also make them more susceptible to following and complying with the cult ideology."

"Since Cosette and I are working undercover in Deal, is there anything we can do to maximize our chances of connecting to a cult member...breaking into their inner circle?"

"Definitely! Cults love preying on younger people. Since Cosette is a new high school student at Deal High, she could be someone who attracts attention from them as a potential recruit. The fact that the town believes she is recently orphaned and just moved to town, makes her a prime target. Cults are always looking to increase their numbers. They seek out vulnerable individuals. In their minds, the more members they accumulate, the more power they have. I feel it's critical for Cosette to act meek with her classmates. If she acts bold and confident, it will lower the chances that they'll approach her. She should behave as if she's insecure. Look down often, avoid direct eye contact with the other students. Obviously, it isn't a guarantee that she'll get approached by a cult member but it'll increase the likelihood. Remember, cult members receive accolades and a higher standing in the cult if they bring new members. It's in all of their best interests to bring new recruits. If any high school students are involved in the cult, I'm betting that Cosette will get approached."

"Debbie, this information has been super helpful. I'll brief Cosette on all of this. In the meantime, I'll continue to keep a close eye on the web."

16

FRIDAY NIGHT
BACK TO SCHOOL DANCE

Cosette entered the school auditorium. Music was blaring and the room was hot and stuffy. Popping a mint to curb her nausea, Cosette scanned the room for her friend-group.

She spotted Winter and Zach first. They were tangled in each other's arms on the dance floor…slow dancing to a Taylor Swift song. The pair looked completely enthralled in each other.

Another wave of nausea hit. Cosette became alarmed and thought, *I can't vomit at the dance. The last thing I need is to bring extra attention to myself. I sure don't want to use the bathroom here. It'll be obvious I'm throwing up. I'll run to the bathroom where my chemistry class is. It's nice and secluded. Nobody will hear me there.*

Cosette made a dash to the building where her Chemistry class was located. The hallways were dark and she used the light from her cell phone to illuminate the way.

Once inside the restroom, she flipped on the fluorescent, overhead lights and raced to a stall. Cosette made it just in time. She knelt on the sticky floor which only increased her queasiness. Her stomach lurched and gurgled.

Finally, she uploaded the contents from her last meal. Cosette's esophagus burned and her eyes watered. Her heavy mascara moistened and sealed her eyes together. The room spun before her.

Just then, the lights from above went out. She froze in terror. Hearing heavy footsteps approaching her stall, Cosette jumped up into a defensive stance. As she did, she detected an eerie scratching noise on the stall door.

"Who's there?" Cosette demanded.

A haunting, deep voice responded. "You're pushing it. You'll be the next one to fill a casket in this miserable town!" The statement was followed by a chilling and sadistic laugh. Fast paced footsteps plodded out of the restroom.

Still bleary eyed, Cosette sprang out of the stall, swung the bathroom door open and attempted to peer around the corner in hopes of seeing who the individual was. There was nobody in sight. She calmed her racing heartbeat and collected herself.

I obviously can't report this to anyone at the dance. I'm working under cover here. They'll wonder why someone threatened me.

After rinsing her face with cold water, she plodded back into the multi-use room, making every effort to appear as calm as possible. Quinn, who was chaperoning the dance, approached her.

Indigo, how are you enjoying your first dance here?"

"I'm loving it. I didn't realize you were chaperoning the dance. It's so great to see you." Cosette complimented the good-hearted teacher with genuine affection.

"Yeah, I like chaperoning and I'm lucky that Jenna doesn't mind that I'm at school events. Some of my teacher friends have kids at the school too. Their children are mortified and protest if their moms want to sign up to chaperone. Jenna encourages me to be here."

"I'm not surprised. Jenna adores you. Heck, we all do."

"The feeling is mutual, Indigo. Jenna and I feel so blessed that you moved to Deal. You're a bright light in our lives. Please know that you can always come to me if you need to talk. I know being new to an area can be trying."

"Thanks, you'll be the first person I come to."

Winter and Zach waved and walked over when they saw Indigo and Quinn.

Zach gently tapped Indigo on the shoulder. "Hey Indigo, we're all going to head to my house for an after-party. We'd love it if you'd join us."

Cosette felt an overwhelming fatigue but was aware that it was critical to the investigation to take part in social activities. She knew that at an after-party, alcohol would likely be flowing. Then, inevitably, the friends would become loose lipped.

"I'd love to go. Thanks!"

Winter chimed in. "Great, we're all heading over in Zach's car. We can drive you home after the party. Do you have a certain curfew?"

"No set time, but, I'm sure my uncle would appreciate it if I got home no later than midnight."

After bidding goodbye to Quinn, the friend-group crowded into Zach's car and sped off to his farm.

The group of friends' laughter echoed into the frigid, night air. They huddled together and walked into Zach's barn. What they saw caused a collective gasp.

A lit candle was laying on the floor of the barn. Zach walked over to it.

"Oh my God, guys...look at these red drops encircling the candle."

Winter's voice quivered. "Uh,...that looks like blood."

Zarina shrieked. "What the hell is up on the wall? Why are there photos of all of us?"

Cosette scanned the scene. She walked over to the photos. First, in the line-up, were portraits of Belle London and Ruth Brownson. Each of their faces had an X drawn across them in black marker.

Next, there was an individual photo of each of the members in the friend group, including Cosette. Zarina's photo was the first one after Ruth's, then Cosette's, Jenna's, Winter's and finally Zach.

The photos of them had clearly been taken at the dance tonight, from a distance. Their names were written on the wall below each of their portraits. Cosette suppressed a horrified gasp when the name under her photo stated, *Cosette.*

Zach pointed to the name, *Cosette.*

"Why would it say Cosette instead of Indigo under your photo?" The friend-group turned to her with looks of bewilderment in their eyes.

Cosette felt the heat rise into her face. She stammered, "I...I don't know. That's so strange." Trying to add some levity to the situation she stated, "I've been called a lot of things in my life but Cosette is certainly not one of them."
The group forced a chuckle.

Zach persisted, "I just don't get why it doesn't say Indigo under your photo."

Just then, to Cosette's relief, the conversation was steered in another direction. Winter chimed in, "Oh no, look! Further down on the wall it said, *Get ready. You're next!*

The group stared silently at the display. Finally, Zach spoke up. "What the hell is this? Somebody snuck into my barn! This is an outright threat!"

Jenna furrowed her brow. "So scary. We need to report it to my dad! I'll call him from outside the barn...cell reception is better out there."

She stepped into the darkness of the night and dialed the sheriff's number.
He picked up on the first ring.

"Hi, pumpkin!"

"Dad, I'm at Zach's house. Can you please come over here? Something super creepy has happened. There are photos of all of us on the barn wall, plus, pictures of Belle and Mrs. Brownson. A threat is written next to the photos."

"I'll be right there, sweetheart. Stay together until I get there."

Jenna went back into the warmth of the barn. Her friends were huddled together. Indigo raised a brow when she walked in. "Were you able to reach your dad?"

"Yeah, he's on his way. Should be here in about five minutes. He told me that we need to stay together."

"No arguments from me." Zarina chimed in. "I'm super spooked. Do you think the killer of Belle and Mrs. Brownson did this?"

"That's pretty much what it implies." Zach stated. "And, who was taking pictures of us at the dance? I didn't see anyone. Talk about creepy."

17

Sheriff Booker parallel parked on the dusty, country road and darted into Zach's barn. The friends let out a sigh of relief when they saw him.

"Dad! Thanks for getting here so fast. Look at this!" Jenna pointed to the collection of photos on the barn wall.

The sheriff went over to inspect the display more closely. As Jenna had described, there were photos of both murder victims with an X viciously slashed across their faces.

Then, he noted a line-up of photos of the friends. Next, he inspected the candle and the red spots on the floor. The sheriff was alarmed when he noticed that the name *Cosette* was written under his undercover agent's photo. Everyone in town knew her as Indigo. This was a clear message that somebody *was privy to the fact that Cosette* was working undercover as a high school student.

If he had to guess, the person who was aware of this highly confidential fact was more than likely the killer.

"Y'all, I'm gonna need you to stay away from this area. I have to test the red stains on the floor. Don't want the area contaminated. Zach, are your parents aware that their barn has been vandalized?"

"Not yet, Sheriff. They should be home soon though."

"No problem. I'll ring your dad's cell and tell him what happened. In the meantime, I'd like all of you to stay away from this area. It could just be a prank but it could also be a legitimate threat. Head on inside the main house or you can all come over to our place."

"I think we're going to head back to our place, Dad. I can't speak for everyone but I'm feeling pretty unnerved."

Winter and the rest of the group nodded in agreement. Cosette had been taking mental notes of the scene and the friends' reactions. She was eager to see if the spots on the floor would test positive for blood. Her gut was telling her that this was a true threat rather than simply a prank. It was particularly daunting that her real name was written on the wall.

Sheriff Booker escorted Zach into his home and, after a thorough walk through, told him to keep all the doors and windows locked until his parents returned.

He, then, drove Indigo, Winter and Zarina back to his house with Jenna in tow.

Quinn was waiting for them with steaming cups of hot cocoa upon their arrival.

"Girls, I heard that Zach's barn was vandalized and your photos were up on the wall with a threatening message. Everything will be okay. Sheriff and I would never let anything happen to you. Here, I made some hot cocoa. Let's sit around the fireplace. It's cold out there."

Jenna chimed in. "You're the best, Mom."

The rest of the girls nodded in agreement. Quinn had a way of calming everyone. She was a bright light in an otherwise daunting and dark world.

The girls huddled around the cozy fireplace. Once everyone had a cup of cocoa, Quinn sat down with them.

"How are y'all feeling?"

Jenna responded first. "We're scared, Mom. The pictures of us on the wall were clearly taken at the dance tonight...from a distance."

Quinn sat and appeared pensive. "Did any of you ever see anyone tonight with a camera? I know I didn't...except for students from the yearbook class. But, that's standard. They're always at events taking photos. I'll go to their class on Monday and try to see what photos they took at the dance tonight. I'll swing by the class unannounced first thing in the morning. That way, if anyone there is up to something shady, they'll be caught off guard with my impromptu visit."

"That sounds like a great idea, Mom."

Quinn continued, "Listen, ladies, I know there's been a lot of uneasiness around Deal lately because of the murders. I'm sure the vandalism tonight didn't exactly ease your fears. You're never alone. Please know that. You can always come to me if you feel worried or if you're nervous about going somewhere alone."

Zarina sighed in relief. "That means a lot to us. You've always been like a second mom to me. Knowing that you're at school also makes me feel calmer."

"That's what I like to hear, Zarina. Cows will fly before I'd ever let any of you get hurt. Winter, your cocoa is looking a little low. May I give you a refill?"

Winter giggled. "You read my mind."

They spent the remainder of the evening playing board games by the fireplace. At the end of the evening, Quinn drove all of the friends safely home.

Cosette let out a sigh of relief when she got back to her rental home. Tommy had fallen asleep and was sprawled out on the sofa in front of the blaring television. He startled when Cosette burst into the front door.

"Yikes! I must have drifted off. What time is it?"

"It's after midnight. I sure have lots to tell you."

"What happened?"

"While at the dance, I had to throw up. I obviously didn't want to bring more attention to myself and use the multi-purpose bathroom. So, I went to another wing of the school. Mid-vomit, the lights went out in the restroom. Then, a deep, male voice, right in front of my stall barked, "You're pushing it. You'll be the next one to fill a casket in this miserable town.""

Tommy's face blanched. "What? This is really serious. Somebody knows you're undercover, obviously, and they know you aren't who you claim to be. We need to report this to the sheriff and to our department."

"I agree. Unfortunately, there's more. After the dance, the friend group and I went to Zach's house. They wanted to party in his barn. When we got there, there was a candle lit, and red drops around the candle which was probably blood. The Sheriff is going to test it. The worst part is that there was a display of photos up on the wall of the barn. The first photos were of Belle and Mrs. Brownson. Then, there was a line-up of pictures of Zach, Winter, Jenna, Zarina and even my photo. Here's the worst part. Each of our names were written under our portrait. I'll let you take a wild guess. What name do you suppose was written under mine?"

"Please tell me it said Indigo!"

"Nope, it said Cosette! I was sweating bullets. Luckily, they only asked me a few questions about why that name was written under my photo but then they dropped the subject. The words, "Get ready! You are next," were scribbled on the wall. Jenna called her dad right away and he came to inspect the area."

"I don't like this at all. Writing your true name is clearly a threat and a message that somebody is on to us. And, there's a high chance it's the killer or killers. I'm glad the sheriff is testing the drops to see if it's blood. It definitely should serve as a reminder to us how serious and risky it is, especially for you, to work this undercover assignment."

"I'm glad we're going into the weekend now, Tommy. We can head up to Reno and have a meeting with your dad about what our next steps should be."

"Yeah, I could see Dad possibly pulling us out of here. The one thing he won't want to do is continue to leave you in such a high risk situation."

Winter was just starting to drift off when she heard a tapping sound coming from her bedroom window. She startled, bounded to the curtain, and peered out. Since her bedroom was on the second floor, she had to look down towards the ground.

A smile spread across her face when she realized her late-night visitor was Zach. He had been throwing small pebbles against her window in hopes of rousing her. His plan had worked!

Winter cracked her window open and she felt a frigid gust of wind blow against her skin.

Unable to disguise her delight, she called out to him. "Zach, what on earth are you doing here? To what do I owe this pleasure?"

Zach's smile broadened from ear to ear. "Well, I just happened to be in the neighborhood and I figured I'd come visit my favorite girl."

Winter giggled. "In the neighborhood? You live clear across town and it's after one in the morning."

"Ok, I'll fess up. I can't stop thinking about you. You're on my mind twenty-four hours a day. Is there any way you could sneak out? I brought booze and some of your favorite foods. We could have a picnic in the forest."

"Oh, sweetie…you don't need to ask me twice. Pretty sure my parents are fast asleep. I'll be down in a minute."

"I was hoping you'd say that, baby. I have blankets but bring a thick coat too. It's cold as anything out here…feel like I'm on the frozen tundra."

"Will do. Be right down."

Winter's heart was pounding. She had been dating Zach for a relatively short time, but she was crazy about him.

She pulled on her scarlet-red coat, tiptoed down the stairs and ran into Zach's waiting arms.

He pulled her close to his broad chest and then they began to kiss passionately. Winter melted closer to him.

"Come with me! I know the perfect place to set up our picnic."

"I can't tell you how excited I am to see you, Zach, but I'm a little spooked to be out here at night after the vandalism in your barn. Are you sure we're safe?"

"Of course! I would never let anything happen to you. Plus, there's safety in numbers."

"I agree, and it sure doesn't hurt that you're the tallest and most muscular boy at our high school." Winter blushed and was relieved that it was too dark for Zach to see her reddened cheeks.

They walked hand in hand along the moon-lit trail. When they reached a clearing in the woods, Zach unfolded a large, blue checkered picnic blanket and placed it on the forest floor.

He motioned to Winter. "Have a seat, baby."

Once seated, Zach pulled out two plastic cups and poured the eighty proof alcohol.

"I'd like to make a toast...to our relationship and to the first of many more picnics together."

They clinked their glasses together and snuggled up close to each other. An owl serenaded the couple with his gentle call. Zach pulled Winter close to him. They stared at the blanket of stars. A shooting star danced across the heavens.

After some time, Zach interrupted the silence.

"Winter, I've been meaning to talk to you about something for a while now."

"Oh, no? Should I be worried?"

"No, not at all. I'm hoping you'll think what I'm about to tell you is a good thing."

"I'm on pins and needles."

"The truth is that I've enjoyed our time together a lot. I love dating you."

"I feel the same way."

"I would like more now. I want you to be my girlfriend. Dating is great but I was hoping we could kick it up a notch...be exclusive."

Winter was so touched by his words that she had to suppress tears.

"You've just made me the happiest girl in the world. I would love to be your girlfriend."

Winter leaned in and they kissed so intensely that they both had a difficult time catching their breath.

The hours flew by. At four in the morning, Zach walked Winter back to her house. They embraced a final time before she headed toward the sliding door.

"Winter…I'm falling hard for you."
Her pulse quickened. "I'm falling for you too."

Winter tiptoed back to her bed and snuggled under her fleece covers. She kept replaying in her mind the moment Zach said he was falling for her.

She fell into a deep, peaceful slumber, feeling happier than she had ever been before.

18

The following morning, Cosette and Tommy met Frank in a conference room at the Reno Police Department.

Frank greeted them warmly. "There's a heck of a storm out there. I was worried about your drive up here."

Tommy responded. "It was smooth sailing, Dad. The traffic was stop and go but we still made it here on time, somehow."

"Well, I'm glad, Son. Have a seat. Can I get you some coffee?"

Cosette and Tommy both declined. Frank continued the meeting.

"Needless to say, I'm not thrilled that someone threatened you in the restroom at the school dance, Cosette.

Furthermore, Sheriff Booker updated me about the vandalism at Zach's barn last night. He told me that, under your photo, the name Cosette, rather than Indigo, was written. Before, we even get back the test results of the red drops on the barn floor, I can tell you, without a doubt, that this was not some random kids vandalizing. Whoever, wrote your true name under your photo, is more than likely the killer."

Cosette suppressed a shiver. "I was thinking the same thing. I've been pretty nervous ever since this happened. Somebody is on to my undercover assignment."

"I've been giving our predicament a lot of thought. I'm thinking it's time to pull you and Tommy out of your undercover assignments. It's just not worth your safety."

Cosette rubbed her temple.

'Frank, I have a proposal. I know we all agree that the killer probably knows that Tommy and I are undercover cops but the friend group at Deal High, more than likely, thinks that I'm a legit student. I've made great progress at Deal High. If we pull out now, we basically have nothing...but, if I continue to work undercover, I'll only get closer to the students. I'm convinced we can get some valuable clues from one of these students. It's a small town. Belle London was one of their peers and a pretty close friend to them. Somebody knows something. I just know it."

"Hmm, it makes me nervous to send you both back, but, I do see your point. Okay, let's continue to have you both work undercover there. We can review again in a week or so if we feel it's still a good idea."

Tommy and Cosette gave each other a high five. Tommy turned to his father.

"Dad, can I take you out to lunch?"

"I'd love that! Shall we go to the Petey Pork Diner?"

"My very favorite place, the ribs are to die for. Cosette, care to join us?"

"I would, but, I need to go see Spencer and Luke. I've missed them so much."

"Of course, partner. Take the car and we can meet back here tomorrow morning. That way you don't need to rush back to Reno and you can spend some time with your family."

'Sounds like the perfect plan. I'll hit the road now. You two gentlemen have a wonderful afternoon together."

VIRGINIA CITY, NEVADA

Cosette called Luke on the drive to their home. He picked up on the first ring.

"Cosette, tell me you're on your way here. I've never missed you more and Spencer is going crazy to see his mommy too."

"You bet I am, sweetheart. I just left Reno about five minutes ago. GPS shows I should be there in about an hour. There's a little traffic, so, bear with me."

"You're worth the wait. Just drive safely. We have the rest of our lives together. An hour won't make or break anything."

Cosette bounded into their home. Spencer screamed. "Mommy!" He wrapped his arms tightly around her waist. Luke appeared in the entry hall moments later.

"Cosette, how I've missed you!" He pulled her close to his chest. She melted and sighed with pure happiness.

Luke continued. "You must be hungry? I ordered your favorite dishes. Let's all go to the dining room."

Their fingers entwined as they headed for the stately eating area.

Spencer sat on one side of Cosette and Luke was on the other. The dining table was filled with steaming plates of pork fried rice, Kung Pao chicken, mango prawns, and Mongolian beef. Her mouth watered.

"My morning sickness has gotten much better. Thank goodness! I can actually enjoy all of my favorite foods again."

"I can't believe you're in your second trimester now. You're glowing...more beautiful than ever."

Luke leaned over and gave her a tender kiss.

Spencer chimed in, "I' can't wait to see the baby. I hope it's a boy. I want a brother to play baseball with."

Luke furrowed his brow "Girls can play baseball too, buddy. Besides, whether it's a boy or a girl, our baby will be loved to the moon and back."

Luke turned to Cosette. "I'm happy we've decided not to find out the gender of our baby. It makes the pregnancy even more exciting."

"I agree. I'm on pins and needles. My ultrasound is next month on the twenty-second at 1:00. I hope you can be there?"

"I wouldn't miss it, sweetheart...and Spencer will be there too."

"Yay, I love to see pictures of my brother or sister. Even though it looks like a blob...it's still fun."

"Cosette, we have missed you more than I can possibly say. I've been worried about your safety but once you told me the killer probably knows your true identity, I've been close to frantic. It mortifies me that your real name was listed under your photo in that barn."

"I know. It scared me to death."

"How did your meeting with Frank go? I'm assuming you're getting pulled out of your under cover assignment. We finally get to have you back home." Luke's entire face lit up with sheer joy.

Cosette felt a lump form in her throat. She stalled. "Uh...the meeting with Frank was helpful. He did think that Tommy and I shouldn't work under cover in Deal anymore."

"That's the best news I've heard in a long time. Frank's a reasonable man. I knew he'd never put you or his son at risk."

Cosette bit down nervously on her lip.

"Actually...I disagreed with him. I feel that I've made far too much progress at

Deal High to stop now. My connections with the students are deepening. I'm convinced that somebody there knows something. We can crack this case if I hold on just a little longer."

"What?" Luke's cheeks reddened to a scarlet-red shade. "Tell me you're kidding!"

"No, Luke. I'm not."

Luke looked at Spencer. "Buddy, your mom and I need to talk. Since you're finished with your lunch, why don't you go play out back. I'll call you when dessert's ready"

"Sure thing...I'll go play in the sandbox."

Spencer dutifully exited the room.

Luke cleared his throat. His eyes were wide and filled with anger. Cosette had never seen him like this before.

"Are you seriously going back to Deal and put, not only yourself, but our baby in jeopardy?"

"I'm going back but I would never make that choice if I believed I was in harm's way."

Luke's voice raised. "Make that make sense, Cosette! There's a mass murderer out there. He knows that you're not actually a high school student. He somehow figured out that you're working undercover. The cover is blown now. The assignment is over! End of story! How in the world do you not think you're in danger?"

"I'm trained at my job. This is what I do. It's my career. Not to mention that I have my gun on me at all times."

Luke snapped. "You promised me before you left that you would never put you or our baby at risk. If you choose to go, you are breaking your promise to me. Don't go!"

Cosette suppressed tears. Her lips quivered. "Luke, I promise you that I won't let anything happen to me. Every day that this monster isn't caught, is a day that another innocent life could be taken. As an officer of the law, it's my job to do everything possible to protect the public. Please, understand. You know how much I love you and our family. I'm getting to the point where students at the school are confiding in me. If I pull out now, we'll have lost everything."

"If you return to this assignment, I'll have no reason to trust you anymore."

"Don't say that! You're my world!"

"Actions speak louder than words. Trust is key in a relationship. You went back on your word. I'm starting to think you aren't the woman I fell in love with. Enjoy your afternoon with Spencer. I'm outta here."

Luke stormed out of their home, slamming the front door. Cosette heard his

sports car racing away. She collapsed
onto the floor.

19

FALL FESTIVAL, DEAL, NEVADA

Jenna, Zarina, Winter and Zach entered the annual Deal Autumn festival. The energy in the air was infectious. Temporary rides and food stands were in abundance. The friend-group ordered cotton candy and continued to walk around.

Zarina pointed. "Guys, look! There's a stand over there with a tarot card reader. I've been wanting to get my future read."

Winter chimed in. "I have too! Let's go."

The foursome went and stood in line. A middle-aged couple who was in front of them in line turned backwards and looked at the friends. The woman of the group stated, "I normally don't believe in psychics but I've heard that this psychic has actually even helped out the FBI with murder cases!"

Zach gasped. "Really? I've always been a skeptic too but that's really cool."

The woman continued. "Yeah, this psychic told the Bozeman, Montana police department exactly where a missing person was buried! She took them straight to the tree. Sure enough, the body was buried where she said it would be. She's the real deal. Her name is Sophia Perez. She's good friends with our mayor. She attends our festival every year as a favor to him."

Winter's interest was piqued. She had always wanted to do a tarot card reading but it was even more exciting since this lady had helped the FBI.

When it was finally their turn, Sophia called them into her tent. There were several seats surrounding her desk.

"Have a seat, please. Who wants a reading today?"

Winter and Zarina both raised their hands. Sophia pointed to Winter. "Why don't I start with you."

With a lump in her throat, Winter sat down in the chair across from the psychic.

Sophia drew a number of cards. "These cards are meant to bring you guidance, messages and answers." She placed cards onto the tables and stared at them thoughtfully. "Okay, I see a new romantic relationship blossoming."

Winter blushed and looked over at Zach.

"The tarot card reader continued. "I see that you have had a fresh start recently. Is this true?"

"Yes, I just moved here."

"I feel a great deal of happiness and love surrounding you."

Sophia continued her reading with Winter. Everything she said about her life seemed accurate. It was Zarina's turn next.

"Come into the hot seat, dear." Sophia motioned for Zarina to sit across from her.

After some small talk, Sophia shuffled her cards and began to place them on the table. The friends heard the psychic gasp as she gazed down at the cards. She tried to compose herself. The room was awkwardly silent.

Zarina pressed, "Is everything ok, Sophia?"

Sophia hesitated. "Um, I'm having a hard time reading your cards."

The psychic's face flushed to the shade of a ripe cherry and her eye twitched. "Why don't I give you a refund, dear. I apologize. My cards seem to be…glitching."

Zarina was clearly startled. She subconsciously tugged at her angel pendant. "Wow, have you had this happen before?"

"Sure, dear." The psychic responded in a hesitant and unconvincing tone.

The friend group exited the tent. Zarina's normally statue-like posture was hunched.

Winter walked next to her and flung her arm soothingly around her friend's shoulder. "Zarina, try not to let the incident with the psychic bother you. I'm sure it means nothing. Besides, these readings are just supposed to be fun…like party tricks. Don't take it too seriously, girl."

"You're right. I'm being silly. Hey, I have an idea. I heard the haunted house is amazing this year. Shall we go?"

Zach's face lit up at the suggestion. "That sounds like a great idea. I love haunted houses. Let's go."

Jenna chimed in, "My mom is actually volunteering at that exhibit. It'll be fun to see her."

The line to enter the haunted house snaked around past the corn dog stand. The carnival was packed. The large number of people waiting reminded Winter of an ant hill...hoards of individuals headed in every possible direction.

Zach entwined his fingers with Winter's. Her pulse quickened. Their whirlwind relationship was nothing short of thrilling. She was crazy about him. Zach treated her like gold. They had gotten to the point where they were essentially inseparable.

Winter loved Linden, New Jersey. It had been difficult for her to leave the town she had grown up in. Her friend group in

Deal had made the transition pain-free. She felt as if she had lived in this new town since birth.

As the group of friends approached the entrance of the haunted house, they spotted Quinn. Her face lit up when she saw them and she waved.

"Hey, kids! I was hoping I'd bump into you. I'm the ticket taker so I figured I'd catch a glimpse of y'all."

"I'd never miss the haunted house, Mom. Especially since I knew you were working it. Looks like you've been busy?"

"Heck yeah! The line has been never ending. It's been a big hit, for sure."

Winter could see strobe lights flashing and loud, eerie music playing. The windows were dark and filled with menacing shadows. Cock roaches were skittering across the cobweb covered entry. A sickly, pale colored mist shrouded the structure.

Finally, zombies motioned them to enter the house of horrors. The contact lenses they wore made them look expressionless and ghoul-like.

The group entered and they could hear the wobbly floorboards creak. Winter grabbed onto Zach's shoulder. "This is the creepiest thing I've ever seen. It's way more realistic than the carnival's haunted house we had back home."

"I know. I never get used to it. It gives me nightmares for days after."

A group of clowns jumped out of the shadows. Winter's skin became covered in goose bumps. Zarina screamed and clutched on to Jenna.

The next part of the house of horrors turned into a dimly lit maze, full of twists, turns and dead ends. People dressed up as insane asylum patients, zipped back and forth between them, creating a commotion. The friends became separated and went down different paths.

Winter felt overheated and her pulse was racing. She wanted to reach the exit. The screams in the maze were ear splitting. Glancing at her Smart Watch, she saw that her pulse was 148...much too high considering her slow movements. Sweat trickled down her tense face.

Finally, Winter was able to spot the exit door. Wiggling past a few more psychopathic looking clowns, she was able to escape into the night. A wave of relief washed over her and she gasped for air.

Jenna burst out of the exit next.

"God, Winter, that was way more intense than last year. Kind of freaked me out."

"I'm glad it wasn't just me. I assumed I was just being a chicken. That house of horrors was a whole different level than what I saw back in Jersey. Yikes! I'm going to have nightmares tonight. I guess Zach and Zarina are still in there?"

"I think so. We all went in different tunnels soon after we entered the place."

Finally, Zach came out of the exhibit. Winter wrapped her arms around him. "Zach, I know you're a tough guy but didn't that exhibit creep you out a little?"

Zach chuckled. "Maybe, a little. They definitely amped up the fear factor from previous years."

Jenna peered around the area.

"Zach, did you see Zarina in there?"

"Nah, I lost track of all three of you almost immediately. She hasn't come out yet?"

Winter took another glance around. "Not yet. Unless she got out before we did and went off to get some food or went to the bathroom."

Zach thought for a moment. "You both know how obsessed Zarina is with Halloween and spooky things. She probably got mesmerized by one of the displays and will come out any minute."

Winter pulled out her cell phone. "I'll call her cell."

The phone rang several times, then, went to voicemail. "It's so noisy in there. There's pretty much no way she'd hear her phone ringing. I'm hungry. Let's go grab some dinner. I'll send her a text and ask her to meet us at the corn dog stand."

Zach and Jenna agreed. After Winter sent the text to Zarina, the friends walked to the corn dog stand. Surprisingly, the line was not long. They ordered their meals and huddled together at one of the outside tables. The wind felt icy.

Zach pulled Winter close to him and whispered in her ear. "Have I told you in the last hour how much I love you?"

Winter giggled. "You have but I can never quite seem to hear it often enough."

Winter had fallen deeply in love with her boyfriend. Not only was she in love with Zach but he was also her best friend. For the first time in her life, she found someone whom she could be completely herself with.

Winter sighed and nuzzled her head up against his muscular shoulder.

Jenna laughed. "You two make me sick. Talk about making me feel like a fifth wheel."

Winter retorted. "Jenna, you're anything but a fifth wheel...hope you know that."

20

As Winter, Zach and Jenna were finishing their dinner, they saw flashing red and blue lights. Sirens were blaring. An ambulance and the sheriff's car screeched to a halt in front of the carnival entrance.

Winter watched the sudden flurry of activity. "What's going on?"

Zach thoughtfully responded, "Maybe an elderly person isn't feeling well. Even though it's far from hot today, all the activity could have made them sick."

Paramedics and Sheriff Booker raced past the corn dog stand and darted over to the haunted house. Winter shook her head. "I bet somebody fainted. That exhibit was boiling hot inside. Let's go see what's going on."

The friends sprung up, weaved through the crowd and made their way to the haunted house. A crowd had gathered. Winter could see the paramedics tending to someone laying on the ground. On the outskirts of the crowd, Winter saw Quinn. She was huddled on the ground and crying. "Jenna, your mom is over there. She looks devastated."

Winter's stomach cramped. The friends raced over to Quinn. Jenna embraced her mother. "Mom, what happened? You're scaring me."

Quinn's face was tear streaked and ghastly white. She tried to speak but she was shaking so uncontrollably that she was momentarily unable to speak.

The friends patiently waited for her response.

"It's…uh…Zarina!"

"What happened, Mom? Did she faint because of the stale air and the heat in the exhibit?"

Quinn wrapped her arms around herself with the intent to self-soothe. "I don't know what happened but...she's...dead!"

The friends gasped and began to sob.

Winter finally blurted out, "What happened?"

Quinn took a deep, raspy breath. "Zarina was found unresponsive. Somebody working inside the haunted house found her sprawled out in a corner. He carried her out through an exit and immediately called 911. Just looking at her, it was clear that she was...dead"

Quinn broke down into a deluge of tears again. They all huddled together in an attempt to comfort each other. Winter leaned against Zach. Everything was spinning around her. She felt as if she was about to faint.

The coroner arrived and the crowd parted. With assistance from the paramedics, Zarina was removed. A white sheet was draped over her lifeless body.

Sheriff Booker lumbered over to them with his shoulders slumped. Quinn wrapped her arms around him and wept.

"Dad, what happened?"

Clearly trying to evade the question, he answered flatly, "The coroner will do an autopsy. This is just devastating. Zarina was a great girl. I know how close you all were to her. I just have no words. I need to head over to her parent's house immediately before they hear it from someone else. This is the worst part of my job."

CORONER'S OFFICE

Samantha Dillon was hunched over the cold, steel examining table, rubbing her temple in a futile attempt to ease the migraine which was beginning to take hold. Dr. Dillon had been a pathologist for over a decade. Until the recent rash of murders, she was accustomed to more run of the mill causes of death..heart attacks, car accidents, an occasional drug over-dose.

As the pathologist pulled Zarina's sheet back, she spotted scratches and abrasions on her face and neck. Her mouth was bruised and swollen. Rope burns and scratches cut into her throat.

After a cursory exam, Dr. Dillon drew blood, tissue, and took small samples from her organs. Once the autopsy was complete, she called Sheriff Booker.

The Sheriff answered. "Hi, Dr Dillon, how's it going with the autopsy?

"You'll need to sit down for this, Sheriff..."

The sheriff wearily slumped into a nearby chair and stated, "Ok. What's the verdict?"

Dr. Dillon took a deep breath. "Based on my initial examination, it's obvious that Jenna was strangled to death. Her death was definitely not an accident. This is another homicide. I'm testing residual fabric within the ligature wounds in order to determine what she was strangled with."

The sheriff sighed. "Why am I not surprised? This monster is going to keep killing our citizens. He or she killed our other two victims with an ax. Maybe the assailant strangled Zarina since it is a more silent method. Murdering someone with an ax in a carnival display would create too much commotion. We need to figure out who's doing this."

21

The morning light glinted into Cosette's eyes. Had the fight with Luke last night just been a horrible dream? Reality began to dawn on her and she felt a deep despair starting to set in. The events from the former evening flashed through her mind. Luke, the love of her life, fiancé and father of her unborn child told her that he couldn't trust her anymore. Cosette folded into a fetal position and wept uncontrollably. Just then, her cell phone clanged. Could it be Luke?

She reached for the phone and wearily greeted the caller. "Hello?"

"Cosette? Are you okay? Your voice sounds off."

I'm hanging in there, Tommy. I'll fill you in on everything when I see you."

"Ok, but I have some bad news to tell you."

Cosette braced herself. "What is it?"

"There's been another murder in Deal. Zarina was murdered last night in the haunted house display at the carnival."

Cosette gasped for air. Tears streamed down her face. Once she was able to regain her composure, she muttered, "This just proves to me, all the more, that it's important for us to keep working undercover at Deal High. If we don't, more people will die. I can swing by your dad's house and pick you up in about an hour? If that works for you?"

"Absolutely, we need to be in Deal now more than ever."

Cosette screeched to a halt in front of Frank's house. Tommy was waiting at the curb and hopped into the car.

"Cosette, you look like you didn't sleep a wink last night. What's going on?"

She tried to suppress tears but to no avail. They streamed down her tired face. She instinctively touched her stomach and began to speak. "Things are so bad. My life has been completely turned upside down in the last day. Luke is livid with me. He can't believe that I'm going to continue to work undercover at Deal High. I promised him that I'd pull out of the assignment if things got too dangerous. He said that I'm not the woman that he fell in love with and he can't trust me anymore. Then, he stormed out. He never even came home last night!"

Tommy's jaw dropped. He had always considered Cosette and Luke to have a rock solid relationship. Not only was their wedding coming up but she was also pregnant with his baby.

Tommy was pensive for a moment and then responded. "Cosette, I know how upsetting this must be for you but I don't think Luke is being reasonable. He knows you have a job in law enforcement."

"That's exactly what I think! And, now that dear Zarina was killed, it's more important than ever that we follow through with our assignment! We can't let more people die. I'm praying Luke will come to his senses."

Tommy patted Cosette's shoulder. "I'm sure he will. I know he loves you."

"It sure didn't seem like it last night." Cosette's cries turned into wails. Tommy asked her to pull over so he could take over driving.

"Cosette, it isn't safe for you to drive when you're this upset. I'll drive. You try to rest. When we get home, I'll make you chamomile tea and cookies."

"Ok, thanks." Cosette fell asleep within minutes.

Winter and Zach went to Jenna's home for lunch. The three friends were despondent and needed each other.   Quinn greeted them and embraced them in the most comforting hug that Winter had ever felt. Quinn was like a second mother to the friend group. With Zarina's horrific murder, they all needed her more than ever.

Quinn cleared her throat. Dark bags under her eyes hinted at a restless night. I made some lunch for y'all. Come on into the kitchen and we can talk."

The mourning teens trailed Quinn to the kitchen table. She had made frittatas and a quiche. As beautiful as the spread looked, everyone's appetite was nonexistent.

Jenna began to speak. "I can't believe she's gone...this feels like a never ending nightmare. Zarina had her whole life in front of her. Some monster cut that short. It sickens me to think that we were so close by while our friend got murdered."

Zach nodded in agreement. "I feel the same way. How could this have happened? We were enjoying our time at the carnival and one of our best friends lost her life. Makes me wonder if that tarot card reader saw something daunting."

Quinn chimed in. "Tarot card reader? What happened?"

Zach explained. "Before we went into the haunted house, we went to the psychic. She gave Winter a reading but when it was Zarina's turn, the lady clammed up and sent us on our way."

Quinn gasped. "That's so odd. I didn't know that happened. I'll let Todd know about this. I'm sure it doesn't mean anything but I know he doesn't want to leave any stone uncovered. I'll call him now and tell him."

22

Cosette crawled into her bed as soon as they got back to their rental in Deal. She was feeling weak and heartbroken, more scared and alone than she had ever felt in her life. She was pregnant, had a wedding date set and her fiancé had stormed out on her the following evening. She was also mourning Zarina's death.

Tommy walked in with a tray of steaming tea and freshly baked oatmeal raisin cookies. His brow furrowed in concern.

"How are you feeling?"

"I don't remember ever being in this much pain in my life. I arranged for my mom to pick up Spencer after school and bring him back to the cottage. The way things are going, I can't trust that Luke will pick him up and watch over him."

"I'm glad you're having your mom get him. This is so unlike Luke. He's always been doting and loving with you. I bet he'll come around...especially when he hears that Zarina was murdered. Surely, he will see, then, how critical it is for us to continue our undercover assignment here. If we don't get to the bottom of this case soon, more people will die. We can't pull out of this now when we are making head ways here."

"I agree with you. Maybe I should call Luke and tell him what happened. Do you agree?"

"Absolutely, communication is key. I'll give you some privacy. Why don't you give him a call and try to sort things out."

"Thanks, I bet you're right. We just need to talk."

After Tommy exited the bedroom, Cosette took a deep, calming breath. Her hands were shaking and she didn't want Luke to pick up on her anxiety. She called him and it went straight to voicemail.

A half hour later, she attempted to call him again but the call was put straight to voicemail once again. Finally, she decided to send a text.

I hate how things ended last night. I miss you terribly. One of the girls in my friend group at Deal High was murdered last night at the carnival. I'm sure you can see why it's more critical than ever that I continue and follow through with my undercover assignment. I'd never put myself in any undue danger. I love our life and family too much. Luke, please understand that I've been trained in law enforcement. There's no doubt in my mind that I can help solve these murders while still maintaining my safety. Tell me you understand and support my job. Please? I love you very much. I need you. Spencer and our baby need you.

Cosette hit the send button and stared at her phone. She saw the delivered notice display and then she held her breath praying that she would start seeing the communication bubbles. They never arrived. She cried herself to sleep that night.

Quinn had reported to her husband that Zarina went to see Sophia Perez for a tarot card reading shorty before her demise. Although, generally skeptical about fortune tellers or psychics, the sheriff was aware that this lady had, in fact, helped solve murder cases with the FBI. Plus, the mayor of Deal had always spoken highly of her and counted her as one of his closest friends.

A gentle tap at the Sheriff's office door, announced Sophia's arrival.

"Good morning, Ms. Perez. Thank you for coming on such short notice. Please have a seat."

"Of course, I'm very saddened to hear of Zarina's passing. She seemed like such a lovely, young lady."

"Yes, she sure was. In fact, she was one of my daughter's best friends. My daughter told me that they came to you for tarot card readings prior to Zarina's homicide. Is this accurate?"

"It is. First, I did your daughter's reading and that went smoothly..."

"Ok, what happened when you did Zarina's reading?"

Sophia's face blanched and her eye twitched. "It was just awful...I laid her cards out and I immediately saw that Zarina didn't have a future. That has only happened to me once before in all the years that I've been doing readings. A gentleman had an appointment with me about ten years ago. I saw that his life was about to end. He died in a car accident the following day. My gift is indeed not always a gift…"

"That must be very difficult for you, Sophia."

"It's excruciating and warning people won't do them any good. If their destiny is to pass away, there's nothing I can do to prevent it. In Zarina's case, I drew the Ten of Swords…suspected she was going to meet a violent end."

"That's incredible! Did you sense anything else about her murder?"

"Yes, ever since her homicide, I keep seeing multiple shadows. I'm quite sure there is more than one person involved in the rash of murders. I also keep hearing some sort of mutterings or chants. These murders are targeted and probably cult related. There are more murders to come and women will continue to be the victims. That part I'm sure of! Also, I believe that any suspects you currently have in mind are completely innocent. Look beyond typical town thugs. That's all I can really say for now. I'll let you know immediately if I get any more visions."

"I tend to agree on all counts with what you're saying. Thanks for taking the time to meet with me. Here's my business card, Sophia. If you think of anything else, please don't hesitate to contact me."

"I sure will, Sheriff. We can't let these monsters act again!"

23

CULT CEREMONY

The cult members had been summoned to an alternative forest clearing. This location was approximately fifteen miles north of Deal. The leader believed that, due to Zarina's murder, meeting in the forest in Deal was far too risky. Deal had been crawling with law enforcement lately.

Abbott approached the altar and cleared his throat. His voice boomed and he raised his arms skyward. "Do you feel the power we have achieved since sacrificing that high school girl, Zarina?"

The members nodded in agreement and Abbott continued. "We're slowly but surely becoming the most powerful beings on the planet and it's all because you followed my instructions. Slaying her in the carnival's haunted house display was sheer brilliance. That's the kind of smart thinking I need to continue to see from all of you. I know which one of you sacrificed that girl. I want to thank you personally. Please step forward… "

One of the members approached Abbott.

Abbott raised his arms into the air and began to speak again. "You should be very proud of yourself. It's because of your courage and smart planning that Zarina was able to get sacrificed without a single trace back to our group. I want you to have this as a symbol of my appreciation…it's Zarina's necklace. Keep it in your possession and treasure it always. Items belonging to sacrificed people have the capacity to bring us even more power."

The member took the necklace and bowed to Abbott. "Thank you! I will always cherish this gift from you."

In closing, Abbott stated, "I want us to meet at this location again the night of the next full moon. Is that understood?"

The members said, "Yes", in unison and quietly left the clearing.

Winter had always prided herself on being a morning person. She relished the mornings and usually woke up with an abundance of energy, ready to start the day. This morning was different. She grumbled to herself as the first beam of sunlight hit her weary face. Understandably, her sleep had been fitful. When she did finally fall asleep, she was plagued with nightmares about Zarina.

Winter wasn't sure that her heart would have survived Zarina's murder without Zach's strength and support. He was her rock. She plodded into the bathroom and freshened up. Her eyelids were swollen and her face was red and scrunched from hours of crying during the night.

Winter could hear her mother calling out to her. "Sweetheart, Zach is here."

"I'll be right down, Mom."

She quickly brushed her hair and dabbed on some lip gloss.

She plodded down the stairs, embraced Zach and sunk into his chest.

"Zach, I know I just saw you last night but I missed you so much already."

"I get it! I feel lost when we aren't together, baby. I hate not being by your side...even for a minute. How are you holding up?"

"Well, better now that you're here. I just can't believe that Zarina's gone. It's awful because I'm devastated by her death and, at the same time, I'm scared out of my mind that a homicidal maniac is out there!"

"It's super scary. You know that I'd never let anything happen to you...don't you?"

"I know, Zach...but, the bottom line is that we aren't together around the clock. Neither one of us is truly safe."

"Well, the monster hasn't killed any men yet, so, I'm not too worried about me. It's you we need to keep safe."

24

ONE MONTH LATER
DOCTOR'S OFFICE

"Ms. Dupont, we can see you now." The petite brunette, thirty-something, medical assistant smiled and motioned for Cosette to enter the doorway.

Tommy protectively draped his arm around her shoulder and they entered the examining room together.

It had been a month since Cosette and Luke had communicated. He had completely shut her out. To her relief, Cosette's mother was able to watch Spencer while she was on special assignment in Deal. Hurt had been replaced with anger. Cosette was pregnant with Luke's child and he had completely turned his back on her. Without Tommy's constant support, she would have barely survived the previous month. He had even insisted on accompanying her to today's ultra sound appointment.

"My bladder feels like it's about to explode."

"I know it's uncomfortable but in a few minutes you'll get to see your beautiful baby. It'll be worth it."

"I know. I should stop complaining."

"Hey, you've been through a lot in the past month. You have every right to grumble. But, I can promise you that things will get better."

"How can you be so sure?"

"I'm sure because you are a strong lady and you have a heck of a lot of people who love and support you. We'll all be there for you."

"Don't know what I'd do without you."

"Well, you'll never have to find out."

"Tommy, I texted Luke yesterday and reminded him of the time and location of my ultrasound. He never responded...as usual. I'm praying that, by some miracle, he still shows up."

"I'm praying for you, too. He still has a few minutes. You just never know..."

Cosette's hopes faded as the minutes ticked by. Luke had let her down...once again. She had not cancelled their wedding, yet, in the off-chance that they would reconcile. At this moment, she knew that a wedding was no longer a possibility. He hadn't even bothered to attend her ultrasound.

Their relationship was over. She was acutely aware of this fact now. Cosette decided, then, that she would cancel her wedding after the doctor's appointment.

The stenographer entered the examining room. She was young and full of energy, clearly still in the honeymoon phase of her career.

"Good morning, Cosette. I'm Sylvia. How are you doing today?"

"Other than a full bladder, I'm okay."

"Yeah, I know, that part's no fun. This should take about a half hour. Then, you can void your bladder. Why don't you lie back. I'll start the exam."

Sylvia coated Cosette's abdomen with a warm gel.

"I almost forgot to mention…I'd really rather not know the baby's gender."

"That's no problem. A lot of times, it's difficult to even see the gender but if I do see it, I'll be mindful not to say anything to you."

At first, Tommy and Cosette looked at images that appeared to be just blobs on the screen.

"Here's the baby's heart."

Cosette looked on in amazement and felt a rush of excitement to see her precious baby.

Sylvia sighed. "Look! The baby is sucking his or her thumb."

Tears formed in Cosette's eyes. Tommy sighed. "That's amazing. The baby already knows how to comfort itself... smart baby."

After the appointment, Tommy took Cosette to one of his favorite restaurants.

"I've been going to Tasties since I was a teen. I can't believe they're still in business after all these years. I think you'll really like it."

"Sounds good to me. I'm starting to get a little peckish myself."

Tommy pulled into a crowded parking lot. It was a stormy day and the quaint brick building looked especially welcoming in the dark gloom. The sign, Tasties, was flashing in a bright emerald color.

"I love it already, Tommy."

"I knew you would!"

They entered the restaurant and were immediately greeted by a bubbly, shapely figured young woman. Her lava-red hair tumbled over her shoulders. "Come this way, please. I have a booth by the window for you."

Grabbing two green colored paper menus, the hostess motioned them to follow her.

Once settled in their seats, Cosette perused the menu.

"Any suggestions?"

"I always have their baby back ribs but I know you have been more into sandwiches lately. I'd recommend the Reuben sandwich for you. It's delicious."

"Sounds like it will definitely hit the spot."

Cosette stared out at the storm through the double paned windows. Her thoughts were as dark as this late-autumn afternoon.

"Penny for your thoughts. I know you're troubled when you crease your eyebrows together like that."

"That obvious, huh?"

"Maybe not to others, but, I know you. You're hurting. I'm so sorry that Luke didn't show up for the ultrasound. I always saw him as an upstanding, dependable man. I even understood why he was so worried for you to continue your undercover work while being pregnant...but to completely turn his back on you. That's just wrong. No excuse for his behavior."

"I still can't believe it, Tommy. If you would have told me six months ago that this was going to happen I would have laughed and said not a chance. I never had a doubt that we were going to spend our lives together. I pictured us being two little, old people, next to each other on a porch, in rocking chairs, in our nineties."

Tears filled Cosette's fatigued eyes. Her mouth twitched nervously.

Tommy placed his hand over Cosette's.

"I thought you two would go the distance too. You never know. Things could still rebound, sweetheart."

"Here's the problem. He turned his back on me when I was vulnerable and pregnant. Heck, he even turned his back on Spencer. Thank God my mom was able to take care of my son in a pinch or I would have been in an even bigger mess. How can I ever trust him again?"

"That's true. This has been very painful for you. You should be the happiest ever. You have a baby coming in some months. That joy was replaced by pain and stress. It isn't fair."

"No, it isn't. So, that brings me to a decision I have made. I need to cancel the wedding. It's going to rip my heart out but I know it's time. I've stalled as long as I can. I won't get the deposit back anymore but at least, if I cancel now, I won't be stuck paying for my non-existent wedding."

"It probably is time. I agree. Would you like me to call for you?"

"Thanks, but this is something I need to do myself. But...I'd love it if you were next to me when I called."

"Consider it done."

"I'll call when we get back home after lunch."

25

"Zach, I can't believe you're about to meet Jules. You're going to love her. She was my closest friend back in Jersey. I've been counting the days for her to visit. We had already planned on this trip before I moved here months ago. Jules' visit is just what I need. I've been distracted ever since Zarina died."

"We all have been. On a brighter note, I'm excited to meet Jules too. Any friend of yours is a friend of mine. She'll love the party we are giving for her at Jenna's house. Quinn has gone above and beyond...as usual. The place looks super festive."

"Jules has a weakness for pizza and she loves to socialize. She'll enjoy the party. She's excited to meet all of you... especially you, Zach. You're all I talk about during our face-times."

"Aww, I'm flattered. I hope it's all good stuff."

"Of course, it is, silly! And, thanks for driving me to get her from the airport. Can't stand driving in stormy weather."

"Baby, it's my honor. As I've told you, probably a million times already, I'm happiest when we're together."

Zach reached for Winter's hand. They drove in silence. Winter was amazed how comfortable she was with her boyfriend. She could completely be herself with him. There were sides of her she never even knew existed until Zach had unleashed them.

Zach parked curb-side at the Reno-Tahoe International Airport. Moments later, Winter spotted Jules exiting through the automatic, glass doors, towing her lilac colored, wheeled carry-on. Her wispy ponytail was blowing in the frigid wind.

Winter jumped out of the front passenger seat.

"Jules, over here!"

"Oh my God, Winter!"

The friends raced towards each other and embraced as if they hadn't see each other in decades.

"I can't believe you're finally here. I've been counting the minutes."

"I can't believe it either. My flight was so choppy. The turbulence was terrible. My knuckles were white most of the way…but, it was worth it to get to spend a week with you. Now where's this lover boy of yours?"

"Right over here…in the blue Civic."

"Oh dang, girl…he's gorgeous!"

Winter blushed, "I know. Right? Think you two will really hit it off."

The girls tumbled into Zach's car. Zach's voice boomed with excitement.

"We finally meet! Jules, this is so great! I'm Zach, heard so much about you."

"I've heard a ton about you too. It's awesome to finally meet up."

Winter explained. "Our town is about forty minutes from here. Zach will bring us home. We can rest a little. If you're game, my neighbor is throwing a pizza party for us tonight."

"*If* I'm game? When am I ever not game? It sounds wonderful!"

Cosette made the dreaded phone calls. She cancelled her wedding ceremony and reception. Once she hung up, she collapsed onto Tommy's shoulder and cried.

Tommy tried his best to soothe her but the sadness she felt ripped right through her soul.

"Now, I need to pull myself together. I have to go to Jenna's house tonight. They're having a pizza party for Winter's friend. She's visiting from New Jersey for Thanksgiving break."

"Splash a little water on your face. Nobody will notice that you were crying."

"Another problem I have is that I'm starting to show. Nobody can know that I'm pregnant for obvious reasons. I keep telling them that I've been eating a lot and that's why I look more bloated. With the holidays coming up, that excuse may work for a little while but my days working as an undercover high school student are numbered. I feel that we aren't much closer in figuring out who the killer is. My stress is through the roof."

"I feel the same…seems like we haven't made a lot of headway."

"Well, let's see if the shin-dig tonight brings any clues. You just never know. I'll be all eyes and ears. I doubt that any members of my friend group are connected to the killings but I wouldn't be surprised if they know more than they're admitting to."

JENNA'S PARTY

Quinn greeted the party guests in a striking, emerald-green pantsuit. Her hair was up in an iconic Brigitte Bardot type of bun. Tapping her perfectly manicured, lime green acrylic nails onto the wooden bannister, she called for the group's attention.

"Jenna and I are so thankful that you were all able to come. A special welcome to Jules. We're very excited that you're visiting…finally get to put a face to a name. I'll stay out of your way for the night. Pizza, drinks and dessert are all on the island. If you need anything, I'll be in the master bedroom. Have a blast, folks."

Cosette tried to sneak quietly through the front door. She was uncharacteristically late. It was getting harder for her to dress in a way that concealed her pregnancy.

Tommy, with his usual, unlimited patience, planted himself on the sofa and watched Cosette parade out in at least seven different outfits. In the end, they decided that black leggings and an oversized turquoise and black flannel shirt was the best option. The majority of her other outfits clearly showed that she was pregnant.

The friend group turned to look at Cosette as she entered Jenna and Quinn's home.

She was greeted with a chorus of warm hellos.

"Indigo, I'm so glad you could make it." Jenna waved Cosette over to the contemporary, beige-white leather sofa.

Winter approached. "I'd like you to meet, Jules. Jules, this is one of my best friends here, Indigo. She just moved here at the beginning of the school year so we pretty much broke in a new school together."

"It's so nice to meet you, Jules, and welcome to Deal."

"Thank you, Indigo. I'm just loving it here already."

The friend group enjoyed the meal. The conversation was lively. Their favorite top hundred tunes played.

Cosette excused herself and went to the guest bathroom. Zach was just exiting as Cosette approached. His eyes looked blood shot and his face was unshaven.

Cosette entered the restroom and scrutinized herself in the mirror. She freshened up her lip gloss. A lack of sleep was evident on her face. A vibration from the bathroom sink counter top caught her attention. Looking down, she spotted Zach's phone. She knew it well because his screensaver was a photo of Winter. The phone continued to vibrate every few seconds. Texts were coming in at a fast, urgent pace. Cosette squinted down at the screen. To her shock, the texts were from Quinn!

Are you there?

Zach?

"Meet me in the forest clearing behind my house right after the party tonight.

Cosette stared at Zach's phone feeling completely taken aback. She was fond of both Zach and Quinn but there was simply no innocent reason she could conjure up in her mind for these texts.

Meeting alone in a forest at night? I need to get to the bottom of what's going on.

Cosette pulled out her cell phone and immediately texted Tommy.

I went into the bathroom just now at the party. Zach had left his cell on the bathroom counter. I'm seeing texts coming in from Quinn! They are planning on meeting in the forest clearing behind Quinn's house soon after the party ends. I'll text you when I think the party is winding down. Please meet me there! We need to figure out what's going on

Just then, an intense knock sounded on the door. Zach called, "Indigo, I think I left my phone in there!"

Cosette quickly placed her own cell phone back in her bag and opened the bathroom door.

Zach's face was red. He was clearly flustered.

"Hey, did you see my phone?" His voice was clipped and urgent sounding.

"I just saw it now when you knocked on the door. I guess I'm not the most observant person."

Zach's eyes seemed to bore right through her. He snatched his phone off of the counter and went back to the family room. Cosette followed.

Zach seated himself next to Winter and pulled her close to him, kissing her on the neck repeatedly. Winter purred and kissed him back.

The display made her sick to her stomach. She needed to figure out what those texts from Quinn meant.

The party was beginning to wind down. Winter stretched and yawned. "I think I need to get home, guys. I'm exhausted...so glad we could all hang out though."

Zach sprung to his feet. "I'll walk you and Jules home, baby. I know your house is next door but I'm not taking any chances with a killer on the loose."

"I'd love that, Zach."

The trio bid farewell and left the party. Cosette reached for her phone and texted *'Go time'* to Tommy.

Cosette thanked Jenna for the lovely evening, exited the home and walked down the narrow road. The wind was whipping through the trees. Branches creaked and moaned. Her cheeks felt icy and numb.

Cosette slid into her car and turned the heater on to full blast. Relief flooded her body as the soothing warmth encapsulated her. She texted Tommy.

I'm out in front of Jenna's house. Zach just walked Winter and her friend home. I can't stay parked here or they'll notice me. I'll head to Bullton Road and then walk to the forest area. I'll be sure to stay shielded in the brush.

Tommy, the fastest texter she had ever known, responded immediately.

Heading there now. I'll park a ways away also. Meet you in the forest. Please be careful.

Cosette parallel parked on the isolated road. Confident that she hadn't been followed, she turned the motor off and left the warmth and safety of her car.

Her eyes had adjusted to the darkness. She moved seamlessly along the road and finally entered into the cover of the trees. The clearing was only a couple minutes away. Cosette stayed along the tree-line to ensure she wouldn't be spotted by Quinn or Zach.

As she approached the forest clearing, it was evident that the duo had not yet arrived. She took shelter under some nearby vegetation which afforded her the ideal vantage point of the meet up location.

The glowing, pearl-white moon loomed large. Millions of stars dotted the late autumn sky.

The moonlight illuminated the clearing. Suddenly, Zach entered the area. Cosette ducked lower into the vegetation. Hovering over the light from her cell phone she texted Tommy.

Don't come into the forest. It's too risky. You'll be seen. Zach is already here and looking around. I'll text you as soon as I know what's going on.

A svelte, agile figure entered the clearing. It was Quinn! Cosette's jaw dropped. Quinn raced over to Zach and they began to kiss passionately. They clung on to each other as if they were each other's life preservers.

Few words were spoken to each other. After more frantic kissing, Quinn bid Zach farewell and they left the forest in different directions.

Once Cosette was convinced that enough time had passed and it was safe, she darted back to her car. Tommy was waiting for her.

"Let's just get home, Tommy. I'll tell you everything when we get there. We can't afford to be seen out here at this hour."

"Yes, ma'am. I'll be right behind you."

26

Once safely inside their home, Cosette lowered herself onto the sofa. Her pulse was racing and her palms were clammy.

"I'm worried about you! You look like you've seen a ghost. What on earth happened?"

"Brace yourself. As expected, Zach and Quinn met. The part I didn't expect is that they would immediately start making out!"

"Excuse me? Are you kidding?"

"I wish I was. They're clearly having an affair."

"Wow! Quinn and the sheriff appear to have such a close marriage and Zach and Winter seem completely in love with each other. I'm blown away."

"You and me both, Tommy. There are so many things wrong with this scenario. For one, Quinn is a teacher at the high school. Zach is a legal adult but this whole thing is still so disturbing. Quinn's definitely not the saint we thought she was."

"Yeah, no kidding! As morally wrong as it is, we are here to solve the murders. Unfortunately, knowing about their affair is fascinating but it doesn't bring us closer to finding the killer."

"I've been part of their friend group for a while now. I'm surprised we haven't gotten any leads about the murders. People tend to talk in small towns. Rumors are often founded in some truth. I expected to, at least, hear theories from them by now...but nothing. I've gotten particularly close to Winter. She hasn't lived in Deal for very long, so, not surprisingly, she doesn't seem to know much. But, I'll keep trying."

"Time is running out, not sure how much longer you can work as an undercover high school student in your condition. We can only camouflage your baby bump for a little while still."

"I know. Believe me...and I'm stressed to the max about it. Another thing that's stressing me out, with my bloated belly, is that Winter asked me to be her model. She's in a photography class at school and her next assignment is to take portraits in a natural setting. I promised I'd go with her tomorrow so she can take photos of me."

"That sounds like fun. Who knows, maybe some time out in nature will calm you. How have you been feeling that you haven't heard from Luke? Are you okay?"

"No, I'm far from okay. I never knew my heart could hurt so much."

"I still think he'll come around, Cosette."

"Well, he hasn't yet but thanks for the encouragement. I need that."

Cosette had spent over an hour the following morning doing her makeup. Her foundation was so thick that her fingers could indent the surface if she touched her face. Winter had asked her to wear heavy makeup, so, that is what Cosette did. After adding thick, spidery, false lashes, she took a final glance in the mirror, bid Tommy goodbye and went out to Winter's awaiting car. Unlike the following night, the sky was crystal blue.

"Indigo, you look gorgeous! Thank you so much for agreeing to be my model. My assignment is due after Thanksgiving break so I'm kind of pushing it to the last minute. So stressful…you're a life saver!"

"I'm happy to help. We'll have a blast. I love being out in nature."

"So do I. Sometimes, I still miss Jersey but it's friends like you and the beautiful area we live in that help a lot."

"Agreed! I'm kind of surprised that Jules didn't come with us though."

"She wanted to but she woke up with a bad sore throat so mom encouraged her to just stay home and rest."

"Oh, no…she must be disappointed. Maybe I'll pick up some takeout for her after our photo shoot. I know she has a weak spot for grilled chicken sandwiches."

"Great idea, Indigo. You've got to be one of the most thoughtful people I've ever known."

"You're always so thoughtful too, Winter. Where are we heading to take the photos today?"

"There's a forest about thirty minutes from here. It's gorgeous. There's even a stream that runs through it. I think we'll get some great photos at the location."

Winter parallel parked along a quiet lane. The tires crackled as they crunched over the gravel. Douglas Fir trees surrounded the picturesque area. Their branches swayed in the crisp, autumn breeze.

"Okie dokey, we're here. Isn't it beautiful?"

"It sure is." Cosette sighed and swiped a wisp of hair away from her eye.

"The place I want to take photos at is only about a five minute walk from here. There's a path over to the right, Indigo."

The friends walked along the dusty foot trail.

"I'm glad I brought a thick jacket. This cold breeze is slicing right through me, Winter."

"Totally! Burr. It sure is chilly. I have a pretty clear idea of what photos we are going to take so hopefully we can wrap it up fairly quickly and get back into the warmth of the car."

The friends walked along the shaded path in silence. A bubbling stream could be heard gurgling in the distance.

They reached their destination. It was a magnificent sight. A sapphire-blue stream splashed and sprayed as it meandered through the trees. The water trickled over the rocks. A pair of ducks paddled along the edge. Sunlight filtered through the canopy of trees.

"Wow! You weren't kidding! This place is amazing."

"I knew you'd like it and the lighting is perfect for photos. Why don't you come over here. You can sit on this rock and look down into the stream. I think that should make some award winning photos!"

"Sure."

Cosette removed her heavy down-coat and placed it on a tree stump. She sauntered over to the rock near the stream. Combing her bottled blond hair one last time, she positioned herself onto the large rock.

"That's perfect, Indigo. Now look down into the stream dreamily."

Cosette did as instructed.

"You look amazing! I love it."

Winter snapped a series of photographs, regularly ensuring that the lighting was correct.

Before Winter took additional photos, she stopped and studied the ones she had already taken.

Cosette had a feeling of uneasiness come over her. The silence became deafening and it felt never-ending.

Cosette looked down at the ducks. They seemed so carefree and joyful. She couldn't help but envy them.

At this point, her life had become anything but calm and joyful. She wasn't on speaking terms with the love of her life and she was carrying his child. The stress and sadness she felt on a daily basis was beginning to take its toll on her.

Just then, Winter made a startled sound. "Shhhhhh!".

Cosette's alarm intensified. She whispered "What is it, Winter?"

"I don't think we're alone anymore... Indigo!"

Winter feigned a fearful expression, at first. Then, her eyes bulged and an insane look spread across her face. Cosette suppressed a shiver.

Two cloaked figures emerged from the nearby underbrush.

Winter face turned crimson red as she screamed in the most vicious tone. "I keep calling you Indigo…but that isn't your real name at all? Is it…Cosette?"

Cosette gasped and started to race into the woods. The gun she always carried with her, was contained in an inner pocket of her coat. The coat was still located on the tree stump next to Winter!

Cosette suddenly felt an intense, debilitating leg cramp. It hit her like lightning and she was forced to scramble behind some shrubbery at the edge of the forest clearing.

I'm in trouble! I need backup.

Cosette's mind was racing and her heart was beating out of her chest. She fumbled for her phone.

Tommy needs to know that I'm in danger! He can get here the fastest.

With trembling hands, she started to text him.

Her texting was interrupted.

"Not so fast!" Muscular arms came from behind and grasped Cosette's shoulders with a jolt, knocking the cell phone to the ground. She craned her neck upward.

Terror engulfed her when she recognized her assailants

"Zach? Quinn? What the hell! Let go of me now!"

Cosette began to thrash wildly. Zach's stronghold made it impossible for her to break free.

He snarled. The sound reminded Cosette of a wild animal. They dragged her back to the clearing where Winter was still waiting.

Once they were there, he growled, "You must think we're a bunch of idiots! We've known you're an undercover cop since day one, moron! We know everything about you. You're lucky we didn't slaughter you immediately."

Zach gripped Cosette's shoulder even tighter, causing her to yelp out in pain.

He pushed her to the ground, causing her leg to cramp again. Despite the pain, she felt a sliver of hope knowing that she was now positioned within arm's length of her coat. "

Quinn stepped in. "Since you're about to die and you're so curious-we are a cult and I'm the leader! We killed all of them. Their deaths weren't in vain though. The blood they spilled gave us a great deal of power. We were able to ascend higher in the universe and we are closer than ever in taking over the world!"

Zach interrupted. "When Winter moved here, she became a welcome addition to our cult. Hell, she might be even more cold blooded than the rest of us are." The immoral, power hungry trio cackled.

Quinn continued. "Winter's cute, shy, little, new girl in town act was the perfect cover. Everyone assumed that she was basically a saint. Jenna and Zarina were the only two saints! Zarina's six feet under now, and, after your death, Jenna, my darling step-daughter will be slaughtered next. We fooled everyone!"

A vein in Zach's forehead throbbed. He got closer to Cosette with his ax angled at her forehead. "Cosette, we won't let anyone get in our way. Unfortunately, that's just what you did. You were stupid and now you'll pay for it!"

Cosette touched her abdomen. Her pulse raced and terror filled her heart.

Cosette winced and attempted to pull away.

A deafening shot exploded into the air. Zach stumbled backwards and fell to the ground. Blood oozed from his shoulder. The other cult members were startled and released their grip on Cosette. The distraction allowed her just enough time to grab her gun from her coat. She aimed it at them.

"Don't move or I'll shoot." At the exact same moment, Tommy emerged from behind a bush. "The gig is up, folks. You make one single move and I'll blow you all to smithereens."

Winter and Quinn raised their hands in the air. They knew it was pointless to fight back. Zach writhed in pain and begged for assistance, as blood continued to pulsate out of his shoulder.

Within moments, the trio was cuffed. While cuffing Zach, Zarina's necklace slid out from under his collar. Cosette noticed it instantly and made eye contact with him.

She spit out her words. "You deserve everything coming to you. You all do!"

A squad car and ambulance arrived and carted them off.

27

Cosette embraced Tommy, her eyes filled with tears.

"Tommy, you saved me. Zach was just about to kill me and I foolishly had my guard down. I blew it. I got wrapped up in my friendship with them...very unprofessional and dangerous."

"Don't be so hard on yourself. It's part of being human. Plus, you won't make that mistake again. The important thing is that you and the baby are safe."

"How did you know we were here?"

"I had a weird feeling after you left, call it intuition. Something just didn't feel right. The two of you going off to some remote location to take photos. If all was legit, I would have never let you or Winter

see me. I waited in the distance for a bit…
but, then, I saw Zach and Quinn show up.
I knew you were in trouble."

"I can never thank you enough,
Tommy."

"Hey, we're a team. That's what we
do for each other. I know you'll always
have my back too."

"You've got that right."

ONE DAY LATER

Cosette and Tommy entered Frank's
office.

`He motioned them to have a seat.

"You both look beat."

"We are, Dad." Tommy agreed.

"Cosette, Tommy, I can't tell you how
proud I am of both of you. You wrapped up

the case and handed it to us on a silver platter. You saved a lot of lives. Seems that Quinn was the one calling all the shots in the background. Winter sang like a canary and gave us all the names of the cult members, including Abbot Fields. Quinn was even about to have her own stepdaughter killed next. Blade Florence and Belle's ex-boyfriend, Kurt Tomlin had nothing to do with the cult or any of the murders. The sheriff is crushed. He's on high doses of tranquilizers and he's bedridden. He thought that Quinn was the greatest wife and mom. She fooled everyone. They would have continued adding to the body count. You did good… both of ya."

Cosette was filled with pride. She had solved another case. This was another career milestone for her. She was becoming a highly regarded homicide detective.

"But, as you know, there's never a dull moment around here. There have been three murders of tourists in Carmel, California in the last month. Both of you have been requested to go there and work with local law enforcement to catch the killer."

Tommy grinned. "They are asking us to assist with a case in another state? I'm flattered."

Frank continued. "You both deserve this assignment. I'm not surprised that you were offered the gig."

Cosette clasped her hands together. "Thanks, Frank. We'll make you proud."

"You always do. We will get you settled in a rental home in Carmel or in nearby Monterey. Also, Stella Meyers, a homicide detective from Raleigh, North Carolina, will fly there at the end of the week to join you. We need to move on this quickly. Knowing your track records, I have confidence that these murders will get solved soon.

Cosette was interrupted by the ping of her cell phone. She looked down and gasped. It was a text from Luke!

He had written just four words.

We need to talk.

THE END

Stay tuned for Colleen's next exciting, young adult fiction novelette.

LEGAL BINDINGS

PREVIEW

Emberly Clark craned her neck to watch the meeting through the glass wall, her lilac colored acrylic nails anxiously drummed on the desk.

She could see Paul Cameron standing at the white board. His perfect posture emphasized his broad shoulders and his impressive six foot one height.

Emberly was convinced that he had spent more on his Armani suit than she had spent on a month's rent for her modest, one bedroom apartment.

Emberly and Paul were both classically beautiful people, but, that is where their similarities ended.

Paul was born into wealth. Everything had always come easily for him. Thanks to family connections, he was able to attend Harvard Law School.

Those same connections opened doors for him to work at one of the top law firms in the country. At the mere age of thirty-two, he was face to face with becoming partner at the firm.

Emberly, on the other hand, was raised by a single mother. What they lacked in money, they more than made up for in their close bond.

Her mother, Mandy, after staying out a little too late one night, at the age of seventeen, found out, to her horror, that she was pregnant. Rather than terminating the pregnancy or giving Emberly up for adoption, she chose to embrace motherhood head on. Were there times when Mandy felt overwhelmed and frightened? Absolutely! But, somehow, the mother/daughter team forged forward and thrived.

Mandy worked extra shifts waiting tables at a diner. Combined with earning scholarships, Emberly was able to go to college.

She was now a paralegal at the Wilson and Smithson law firm in San Francisco. She spent her days assisting with case planning, analyzing legal documents and...admiring Paul Cameron.

OTHER NOVELS FROM COLLEEN HLAVAC

I DON'T

THE STALKER IN THE DESERT

LIQUID DECEPTIONS

Colleen Hofstadter Hlavac